DRAGON GIRLS

Dirty Girls Series
BOOK 2

Rodzil LaBraun

Find more novels by Rodzil LaBraun:
Author website: rodzillabraun.com.
Or follow Rodzil LaBraun on Amazon and Goodreads.

CHAPTER ONE:

I gazed across the dark hull of the dormant ship at the carnage, some of which was very recent. Just yesterday I defeated a blue dragon and sent another one flying off with its tail between its legs, so to speak. Of course, Gako's help had a lot to do with my success in that battle. He was the friendly green dragon that had taken to sleeping in the nearest big red tree.

Much of the dead mega lizard's carcass still remained there. Gako hadn't even eaten half of it, which was to be expected. The dead animal was roughly his size. Dozens of alien birds had been feasting on the recent kill that smelled so much like rotting wood. I spotted a few of the smallest dragons getting their share as well, just before we came up to start on exterior repairs. Their lanky yellow scaled bodies were only five or six feet long. Combined with their shorter snout they nearly looked like they could have lived on Earth, in some remote desert.

I managed to cut off a small chunk from the rotting carcass this morning for Vanilla to test. Preliminary results were decent, so the report stated. Hopefully, dragon meat would taste much better than the wofur that had been approved for consumption. I didn't think that we had enough spice on the ship to compensate for its foul odor.

Honeysuckle was currently sexy slender thigh deep into the hull breach in the corner of the spaceship. It was the same section that I had photographed for her the day before. I was no mechanic, by any means. However, I had considerably more muscle than any of the other crew members. That made me valuable when something needed pushed, pulled or lifted. I was waiting for my next opportunity to do one of those things as I scanned the horizon looking for potential threats.

Dead dragons on our roof were less than desirable as they drew hungry flying creatures. However, their obvious demise might just serve as a deterrent to other predators. Perhaps word would spread that a big blue dragon had been slain by a human. Between that and the injured blacks that I had sent on their way, maybe we had started to earn some respect on this planet. Then, as the new guys making noise, it could be that instead we were drawing unwanted attention.

My new sword had undeniably given me improved confidence in my ability to defend myself. I would still prefer a firearm, though. Unfortunately, those needed to be shared by qualified members of the crew. At my suggestion, that list was getting longer. It didn't make sense to me to deprive anyone of the opportunity to register as a shooter. Adjustments needed to be made to the crew's mentality since they crashed on a dangerous alien planet. Rules that had been ingrained in them all their lives no longer applied. It was time to adapt.

I didn't fully understand what Sage and Cinnamon had told me a couple days ago. Growing up on a space station, then enlisting as ship crew limited a person's exposure much more than I had thought possible. In my time these women could be compared with people that had been grown in a lab, given an extremely limited education, and never allowed to leave the building. Ever. They were completely out of their element here and only capable of dealing with textbook scenarios efficiently.

Even more than for my muscle I was appreciated for my ability to think outside the box. Things that were obvious options to me immediately came across as sheer genius when I suggested them. It blew my mind a few times, but I happily reaped the admiration on each occasion.

I had only been an actual member of the crew for a couple days. My attributes, though, sent me skyrocketing up the chain of command. I had been put in charge of all things outside the ship. I only had to answer to Sage, the navigator that ranked highest among the surviving crew members. Strawberry was placed next in line, but she was more like an equal to me, taking responsibility for everything going on inside the vessel. Those were mostly tasks that the entire crew was already familiar with, except me.

Honeysuckle was technically in charge of ship maintenance and repair. She had been trained specifically for the position as a teenager on Infinity Station Vega. Only Sage had a tendency to adjust the mechanic's priorities often. Sometimes it seemed like she was just set on reminding everyone that she was the new boss. Other times her decisions had specific intent. Such was the case when she told Honey not to bother fixing the probe anytime soon. That led to me being sent to the roof to get photos and video of hull damage, which in turn put me in harm's way.

I still believed that Sage had sent me up there to die. My tremendous bravery and shocking success against all odds made her plan backfire. Instead of being dead and out of her hair, I had grown in popularity. As a thorn in her side, I was digging even deeper as the crew began to respect me more than her.

Cinnamon, Coffee and Honeysuckle had all been won over to my side. Not that they were ignoring Sage's commands outright. It was more like they were bending to my will in ways that did not put them directly in a mutinous position. Of course, my contentment to remain under Sage's command for the most part contributed to our situation.

Those three particular women bonded with me quickly for other reasons. Some social, others sexual. We simply got along well. They were helpful in my learning about advanced technology instead of lording their knowledge over me. Managing to bed two out of the three only assisted in my popularity.

I was eager to become the boss. There was no doubt about that. That kind of ambition was part of who I was, how I grew up. But I would compare my situation to a manager that was hired straight out of college to supervise people doing jobs that he had no idea how to do. He could never gain their respect unless he was able to do every job in his business himself. That was what I needed to do before trying to take over. I had a lot to learn. Otherwise, even my precious three favorite girls would stop following me.

Cinnamon had committed to teaching me some valuable things that were not on Sage's list. One or two hours a night in the privacy of one of our rooms I could study everything that I needed to know. It would certainly take a long time that way, but I currently didn't have enough free time to do any more. Every crew member had plenty of work to fill their day.

My tan skinned teacher was easily my best friend among the crew, and the one that had earned most of my romantic interest. Though we spent the previous night together, we did not have sexual relations. In fact, at the pace that we were progressing, it could be quite a while before we did. Unlike Coffee or Honeysuckle, Cinn was in no hurry to get it on. That just made her even more desirable to me.

I knew that I would not have the patience to spend months acquiring the knowledge that would make me a capable commander of the spaceship in flight. But I wouldn't need to. It was highly unlikely that we'd be leaving this planet anytime soon. It would be my superior wisdom and skill in dealing with our destitute situation that compensated for my shortcomings.

"Hey," Honeysuckle called to me from her hole inside the ripped metal of the ship's exterior. I immediately went to her and knelt down for a look inside.

"What's up, Honey?" I asked. She was beginning to make sense of much of my centuries-old expressions. Since the exquisite tit job that she gave me I ranked among those that were permitted to call her by her nickname. When she smiled up at me the memory of that sexual act came back to me.

"I need some parts from inside," she told me. "Cinnamon is pulling them for me. I would prefer to stay in here and work while the supplies are brought to me. How do you feel about that?"

Security outdoors was my domain. She could make the decision on what got fixed and how, but she would have to follow my instructions for getting any parts and tools to and from the entrance which was nestled in the ass crack of the ship.

"Well," I replied. "Obviously, I don't want her to bring them up to us alone."

"She's going to use the anti-grav lifters, so you don't need to worry about their weight or size."

"I realize that," I replied smugly, even though I had not considered it. There were still a few things that these ladies from the future relied on regularly for which I was not yet accustomed. "I'm concerned about her safety getting from the exit to here."

Honeysuckle propped one of her boots up against a busted component just inside the hull. A dark fluid had coated much of it. I wasn't sure if that came from the ship or from the innards of a dragon. She stayed with her set uniform shorts and tight top, at Sage's command. However, she was permitted to use a clear plastic looking overall to protect her fine body during the dangerous work. Those had been stocked for the women instead of normal coveralls so the previous captain and pilot could continue to ogle their lovely shapes as they worked. To me it looked like a failed fashion statement from my time.

"Then, go get her," Honey retorted.

"That would be leaving you alone," I answered. "Duh."

Honey giggled at the use of the last word. It was one that none of them had heard before I came on the scene. It's meaning and intent was easily recognized, though.

"I'm in a hole," she replied. "Nothing will get me for the whole two minutes that you will be gone."

"I can't count on that," I told her. Usually, the strong scented woman would be covered in dirt to mask her dragon attracting aroma. She was relying on her work coveralls to shield it, but I could clearly smell her from a dozen feet away. "I won't take a chance with your life."

"Then leave me the pistol. You have your super sword."

"That sounds like a bad idea, too," I said as I thought about it. I didn't want to risk my life or Cinnamon's either. And honestly, I couldn't trust the mechanic to handle the firearm properly to save her own life should a dragon attack in my absence. "You are just going to have to come with me."

Honeysuckle groaned at my decision. "I hate moving around in this outfit. Besides, if we both go to escort her over here, we'll have to take her back, too. And that is after we climb back up the ladder to get everything where I need it."

I opened my mouth to reply just as I noticed something large in the air out of the corner of my eye. I swiveled quickly and raised the pistol. Fortunately, not only was the large dragon not coming toward us it was also my new friend. The giant green flying lizard that saved my life just yesterday. I hadn't seen him all day. I was relieved when I saw him fly to a perch in the large red tree roughly forty feet off the ground.

"Maybe I could get Gako to come over and babysit you," I suggested to my stubborn friend.

"No, thanks!" she answered quickly. Then she hoisted her slim frame out of the hole. When her sexy ankle boot caught its toe on a jagged edge of metal, she nearly fell onto her face. I quickly reached out to catch her, snagging one arm and one breast in my urgent attempt.

Honeysuckle laughed as I hurriedly adjusted my grip to a firmer less sexual location. "Hey now," she continued to chuckle. She had something funny to say but was struggling to get it out.

"Sorry about that," I told her as I helped her to her feet.

"Well, it is not like you haven't handled them before," she said. "Maybe you could join me in the hole when we get back and play with them again."

I knew that she was joking. Or at least I thought that she was. But the gouge in the armor of the ship was too narrow for me alone. There was no way that we could both fit in there comfortably enough to have any fun.

"I don't think that will work," I replied with a smile.

"Well," she whispered as she pushed her gorgeous body against mine. "You could sit on the side with your pants down, and I could..."

"Hey, Kash!" my communicator cracked to life. It was Cinnamon's voice coming from the small metal tube that circled my wrist like a bracelet. The atmospheric interference made it difficult for them to be used outside. They would only work if both parties were close to the ship.

"I'm at the exit," Cinnamon informed me, sounding a little bit annoyed. "Are you coming to get me or what?"

"Ahh," Honeysuckle said as she pulled away and took a step toward the side of the ship where we would need to descend the ladder. "The other woman."

CHAPTER TWO:

The sun had set uncomfortably early in the day. The expression sounded funny, but it was accurate. We were doing our best to live by the standard twenty-four-hour day for health reasons. The twenty-seven-hour day on this alien planet didn't make it easy for us. We would shorten some days and lengthen others to eliminate a total flip flop of our daytime coinciding with external darkness. But half our days were like this, though sometimes it was dark all morning instead.

Inside the ship it was easy to keep to a consistent sleep schedule. But the more time that we spent outside the harder that it got. As the yellowish sun slipped beyond the horizon the sky slowly transformed from a pale green to a much darker forest color.

Moon number one, as I called it. Or big blue. It hung low in the sky in the direction where we used to fetch water from the murky stream. Baby blue, as I referred to the second one, stayed motionless just above it and to the left. That smaller moon never moved, but you could barely see it during the day. After sunset, the two of them combined cast a shimmering teal glow around them.

An orange moon stood high in the sky on the opposite side. If it weren't so dull, I would have assumed that it was a nearby star instead. That fella only appeared every other night and was completely invisible during the day.

With valuable time left in our workday, Honeysuckle did not want to return inside. She was making much more progress than she had originally anticipated. Against my better judgement I let her continue but forbade anyone else from exiting the ship.

For the first two hours of twilight, the sky still somewhat illuminated by the moons and the stars, I worked to clear smaller debris off the top of the ship. It was not a task that needed doing, but it at least kept me busy. It wasn't like we would be planning to have picnics up there. Keeping it clean served no real benefit. Once the topside repairs were completed, we wouldn't likely ever return to the roof of the ship.

Four recesses were positioned like the corners of a large square, roughly thirty feet in both directions. Wide as a manhole on the streets of Earth, they were less than three feet deep. In the center of each was a loop of pipe thicker than my forearm. I asked Honeysuckle about their purpose as I attempted to clear debris from one using a metal rod from cargo.

"Those are the docking loops," she explained from her position waist deep into the hull breach. "When we dock at a station, they use hooks to grab those and pull us into a stable position."

"You dock with the roof?" I asked. There was no door topside, so I was a bit confused.

"Yes," my green skinned friend continued to enlighten me. "The station spins like a wheel. Centrifugal force creates a pseudo gravity for the people that live there. It also makes it easier to keep objects like cargo in place. Our top hull connects with the floor of the station docks. Walkways, stairs and lifts are then positioned according to the shape and size of the ship. After clamping on it usually takes over an hour before we can exit the ship to enter the station."

I silently gave that some thought as I continued work. This space age that I've transported to sounds fascinating, with its ships and stations, and sexy body modifications. Naturally, I wanted to witness them for myself. However, I was safer and more powerful on this planet. I was even toying with the idea of keeping the ship from ever taking off. Some of my study of how the spacecraft worked could serve that endeavor.

Carefully I pushed what debris I could toward the front of the ship and over the edge. We didn't want junk piled up on the side where we were establishing a base. And I didn't want to shift any weight toward the cliff side to send it off that way. If I could come up with a way to keep this alien world's creatures off that side, I would be able to keep our luxury home stable and secure.

After a while I sat down and simply watched for threats. Reportedly the black dragons were more active and aggressive at night. In low light conditions they would also be harder to see. We used battery torches to brighten up our workspace, but I was hesitant to use them as spotlights. They just might draw more attention to us.

At one point I spotted a pair of eyes shining in the large red tree close by. After staring at it for a few minutes, the dragon that they belonged to, raised his head. Moonlight caught enough of him to lead me to believe that it was Gako. I stayed on alert in case something other than me had woke him. Once he laid his head back down, I leaned back on my hands and yawned big enough that my body shook. Planetary nighttime made me sleepy even if my body wasn't in need of rest.

"Honey girl," I called to my friend working in the hull breach.

"Honey girl?" she replied. Apparently, it was the first time that she had been called that.

"Are you about done for the day? I'm having a hard time standing guard. And it is going to be fairly dark soon at the ground level as we make our way back inside."

"Yes, I think so," she answered, reluctant to stop working. "I'm going to leave most of my tools and parts inside the hole for tomorrow."

When she finally popped her head out and looked at me, I picked up a very strong elfish vibe. Her green skin and white hair caught the moonlight in such a way that she reminded me of a fantasy creature intent on mesmerizing me.

"Do any girls make modifications to their ears?" I asked her as she carefully hoisted her knees onto the hull, waving off my offer of assistance.

"You mean like Vanilla?"

"Vanilla has weird ears?" I asked without thinking about my wording.

"They are not weird, really," Honeysuckle replied. "They are just smaller, flat against her head, and slightly pointed on top."

"Like an elf?" I asked, suddenly excited at the prospect of seeing these ears. I thought back to my close contact moments with Vanilla and was surprised that I hadn't noticed any modifications in that area. Her wonderful full-bodied hair must always shift to cover her ears for me not to notice.

"I don't know what an elf is," Honey said as she rose to her feet. I joined her and helped gather up the stuff that we wanted to take back inside. "Her ear mods aren't that noticeable, especially because of her thick long hair."

"Do other girls make bigger changes?"

Honey laughed before saying, "Yeah, I've seen some extreme mods. Once on Infinity, I saw a bald girl with big ears that stuck out to the side and flapped around when she walked. She looked like a baby elephant."

"Wow!" I got the visual in my mind immediately, but I was surprised that she even knew what an elephant was. Maybe they had zoos on these space stations. Or a new age ark transported two of every earth creature to another planet before our home world became uninhabitable.

"The next time I saw her she had them changed back to normal. Bad mods don't last long unless a person is looking for a negative look."

"Who wants a negative look?" I asked. Then I remembered how certain groups of people from my time did just that. Skin art, butchered hair styles and strange piercings could almost make someone look inhuman.

"Actors," she replied. "People that play villains in the videos. Sometimes security guards have some menacing modifications."

We descended down the ladder carefully one at a time so we could stay alert to anything that might approach us. It was surprisingly quiet around our ship, I thought. The laughing goats must all be sleeping. The wofurs, too. I couldn't stop thinking about all these men and women elsewhere in the galaxy with strange body parts.

"What is the weirdest modification that you have ever seen?" I asked as we made our way toward the entrance.

"Oh, I've seen so many," she replied as she gave it some thought. "I had a friend in school with webbed toes. But they actually looked kind of nice."

"Was she a swimmer?" I asked. That would be a good use for that kind of adjusted body part. It made sense that not all modifications were just for appearance.

"A what?" she asked. I explained what a swimmer was, and she told me that kind of thing didn't exist on stations or ships. Nobody had so much spare water that they could fill a room with it just for swimming.

"I've seen guys with spiked bones poking out of their skin, eyes that spiraled, and hair that looked like leaves," she continued. "But the freakish thing that I saw was a girl that worked on a station supply ship with me. She had a clitoris that was three inches long and jet black."

"What the fuck?"

"Yeah," Honey laughed as we approached the entrance. "She wanted to put it in my butt."

The door to the ship opened suddenly as she finished her sentence. Strawberry stood there to let us in with a strange smile on her face.

"Put what in your butt?" she asked Honey.

"Oh, nothing," Honeysuckle replied, the laughter gone. Those two did not appear to be even the slightest of friends. As of yet I had not heard any reason for the barrier between them.

"Hi Strawberry," I said, trying to stay professional and friendly at the same time. I knew that the red-haired girl would be a pivotal part to the power struggle that was growing between me and Sage.

"Hi Kash," she responded as she stepped aside to invite us in. "Were you trying to put something in her butt?"

"No," I laughed, but cut it short. She stared at me for a long moment, peering into my eyes with a crazy crooked smile. I stood there in silence waiting to see if she was going to say more. Perhaps she was into butt play and wanted to extend an invitation. I wasn't sure what I would do in that situation. She had a freaky Raggedy Ann look going on that might be fun to hook up with, but I was fairly sure that it would not go over well with Honeysuckle. But the redhead's strong scent was an aphrodisiac threatening to weaken my resolve to keep things business-like.

"Huh," Strawberry finally said. When she turned and walked away, I watched her bubbly ass wiggle as she went. It appeared so firm and tight in her uniform shorts. I wondered what her backside looked like naked. And then a funny image nearly made me laugh out loud. I imagined poking her in the ass and causing it to pop like a ruptured ball or balloon. Then I noticed Honeysuckle staring at me with a disapproving look.

"What?" I asked, prepared to deny that I was checking out another girl's rump. Then a thought occurred to me. "Did you want to get together later?"

Honey smiled, but then shook her head. "Not tonight. Besides, aren't we supposed to all meet up soon to discuss building that camp of yours outside the ship?"

"That camp is going to be ours," I replied. "Not mine. And yes, I think we have just enough time for a shower before we get together with the other girls. Would you like to share a stall?"

She smiled once again but refused to dignify my suggestion with a response. Then she walked away. Her walk was much more natural than Sage's or Strawberry's. She was not trying to convey any message. It was just a get from point A to point B kind of thing. But her slender shapely body made it sexy just the same.

I had spent much of the day with her. I thought that it might bring us closer together, but apparently, she'd had enough of me for one day. Earlier she had made a sexual comment in jest. Thinking about what might have changed led me to believe that it was the exchange with Strawberry that turned her off. I would have to be more careful in the future.

That was okay for today, though. I had Coffee and Cinnamon still. I almost expected them to be rushing to meet me on my return inside, like devoted wives. But I should know better. These girls were independent women. A couple days with me wasn't going to change that. A couple weeks or a month? Maybe.

After we put our things away on the lower level I decided to check in on Teddy before heading up for a shower. He was resting with has back toward me up against the bars when I entered. He didn't even bother to turn around to see who had come in.

"Hey Teddy," I said. Still no movement. I hoped that he wasn't dead. "How's it going?" I asked as I slowly approached him.

"Same cage," he replied with his angry voice. Since he always talked like that, I couldn't really judge his emotional state except by his chosen words. "I'm not sure what you think might have changed since your last visit."

"Yeah, sorry about that," I responded. I did hate seeing an intelligent creature caged up without having committed a crime. Unfortunately, I knew so little about him. I couldn't just let him roam free on the ship. I was quite sure Sage wouldn't stand for that either.

Teddy mumbled something under his breath. It sounded like he was calling me a pussy or some other irreverent term. I debated on asking him, but I didn't want things to escalate and cause a wedge between us. He came from a very male dominant society, so perhaps he thought my apology was a sign of weakness. Or my inability to override that woman in charge. I would have to choose my words more wisely in the future. Maybe one day his friendship and respect could make a difference.

"Were they planning on selling you to a public zoo?" I asked.

Teddy turned to face me finally. I got the impression from his triangular koala type face that he was trying to figure out what the word meant. "Private collector probably," he then said. "We'd all be pets for some human."

I glanced at the other two alien life forms and imagined what kind of pets they would make. They looked too dangerous to just let running around free. But then again so did dogs back on earth. Maybe they could all be trained to protect their masters.

"What would any of you do if we were to set you free right now?"

Teddy stared at me for a long time before answering. Perhaps he thought that it was a loaded question and he wanted to word his answer to give himself the best chance of being freed.

"One of these two animals would happily run off onto this strange planet to start a new life. The other would try to kill all of you before it did."

"Woah," I said. It seemed to me that Teddy didn't really have casual conversations. I needed to keep that in mind with future questioning. "Which of them would want to kill us?"

"I'll save that information as a bargaining chip for later," Teddy told me, speaking slower than usual.

Interesting. If I had to guess I would think the Tigritari would be the most vengeful. Basically, a dark green squatty tiger, its golden eyes would study me as it paced its cage. I could picture the Savrad running more gleefully to race to freedom. The colorful lizard had no malice in his eyes.

"What about you, Teddy? What would you do?" I asked, trying my best to not make it seem like an interrogation. "Would you want to remain with us or run off to see if you could survive here on this dragon planet?"

"I've actually been giving that quite a bit of thought lately," Teddy replied as he sat down. His legs were so short that it made extraordinarily little difference in his height when he did. His demeanor and tone suddenly struck me as a narrator for the beginning of a scary movie. But his overall appearance made him look like a talking teddy bear that children would love.

"And?"

"I have haven't decided yet," he said. The smile that crept onto his face was creepy, though I did not believe it to be his intent. A new vibe came to me, one of a possessed stuffed animal. The kind that would slay a family with a large knife.

CHAPTER THREE:

We were twenty minutes into our little meeting when Strawberry appeared in the doorway to the galley. We had decided to use the public setting which was the only comfortable space on the ship for a four-person discussion. There was no reason to be clandestine. The project had been approved by the big ass person currently in charge.

I wasn't sure if the freckled young woman was seeking to use the food processors or was interrupting our meeting. I stopped what I was doing and greeted her warmly.

"Is this a meeting about the base building outside?" she queried.

"Yes," I answered. "Did you need the space for something else?"

"No, actually," Strawberry replied as she tentatively stepped toward me. "I was hoping that I could join in. Would that be okay?"

"That depends," Honeysuckle snapped at her. "Are you going to help us or just get in our way?"

The friendly face that Strawberry was giving me faded quickly as she turned toward my green skinned friend. I should have interrupted to keep things as pleasant as possible with the group, but I was itching to find out what was the problem with these two.

"I have a right to be here," Strawberry told her firmly. "I don't have to ask for permission. I was just being polite. But, for your information, I have no interest in blocking your efforts to expand our habitat outside the ship. Even if the ship doesn't threaten to fall off the cliff there are some legitimate benefits to a secure outdoor workspace."

"I don't have a problem with her sitting in," Coffee announced. I had noticed already that she was the least likely to take offense. Her easygoing personality was much appreciated. She was making it clear that she had no hard feelings toward Strawberry for her being promoted in rank above her.

"Well, she needs to recognize that Kash is in charge here," Honey told her darker friend, instead of addressing the redhead herself.

"Technically," I inserted. "Strawberry can override anything that we plan to do that has a negative bearing on the crew indoors. For example, if we decided to rip all the beds and the food processor out of the ship..."

"That's not possible," Honeysuckle cut me off.

"If it were..."

"I'm not here in that capacity," Strawberry said as she placed one hand on my shoulder. Looking back to me her friendly expression returned. "I'm curious. You have so many brilliant ideas. And I'd like to help in any way that I can."

"And report to Sage with our plans afterward," Cinnamon spoke for the first time since the freckled officer arrived. Her tone and demeanor were calm. She was just stating what she considered to be a fact. We should accept that with Strawberry's presence and adjust accordingly.

"The captain has a right to know..." Sage replied, trying not to be defensive.

"She's not the captain," Honey muttered without looking up.

"Okay, okay," I needed to put an end to this before it really went off the rails. I would have to learn more about the connections between these women later. "This is not being productive. Strawberry is welcome to sit in, as she has a right to do, and report back to Sage as she sees fit. I'll be revealing our plans to Sage at important junctures as well. And she is the highest-ranking officer among us. I don't see that changing anytime soon."

That last part was specifically for the redhead's ears. Only Honeysuckle glanced around to see if anyone was going to disagree. I knew that she particularly was eager to support me in a coup, but the opportunity would not be today. Or tomorrow. Or the next day. Without full support from Cinnamon, I wouldn't even consider it.

"Let me catch you up with what we have discussed so far," I told Strawberry as I motioned for her to take a seat to my left. Cinnamon was on my right and the other two were seated across from us.

I shared the basic layout plan with the new arrival before proceeding with specific construction ideas. My plan was to make an L-shape with the cargo containers that would begin just behind the ship at the exit corridor and wrap around to reach our mist harvesters. Gaps between the units, our new water supply and the ship could be bridged with fences if needed. Then a material could be stretched from the top of the ship in the rear and on the right side to enclose the whole complex.

The hopes of providing a completely secure camp were not realistic. The idea instead was to discourage bigger threats with the somewhat cramp and closed off area, and completely block smaller animals from getting in.

We didn't have enough cargo cubes to make the full L. We would need at least fifty feet of fence constructed using the metal rods. Also, a strong fabric would be needed for the roof. Honeysuckle and Cinnamon combined to list possible components. The whole thing was looking feasible.

I came up with the idea of constructing breakaway hooks to attach the roof to the ship. That way if the space vessel did go over the cliff, or a large dragon decided to land on a section of our fabric roof, we could prevent the whole building from collapsing.

Each individual shared their thoughts and were able to contribute to the overall plan. Strawberry came up with the idea of placing empty cubes on their sides to form tiny rooms for us to use.

"We're still going to need to be covered in the scent block to keep from drawing dragons," Cinnamon stated. "Unless Vanilla can come up with a way to cover the whole complex with something to do the job."

"Can she do that?" Coffee asked excitedly. She hated the fake mud being applied to her skin more than the others.

"I'm sure she can come up with something," Strawberry told us. "We won't want to have to make enough of that dirt to seal everything."

"There is plenty of real dirt out there, too," Cinnamon added. "We can supplement with that where needed."

The discussion continued a while longer before we felt like most of the issues were resolved. Everyone was getting tired and ready for bed. The security of the spacecraft was a very big deal. If we ever lost the ship and had to rely on a structure that we built, a guard would be needed all day and night. We would also have a much more difficult time holding to our twenty-four-hour day. Vanilla said the extra three hours a day could have a huge negative effect on our bodies over time.

When it was just me and Cinnamon left in the galley, I took the opportunity to speak with her privately.

"I'm surprised that you girls have adjusted to life on the planet as well as you have," I told her. "Especially with how you have all had sheltered lives."

"Sheltered lives?"

"I mean being confined to stations and spaceships," I explained. "I'm sure of lot of people would just sit tight and pray for a rescue."

"Well, to be honest," Cinnamon replied. "Most of us did just that. Some of us never went outside for the first week after crashing here. Once the men were killed, we had to step up and pitch in. In fact, it wasn't until after your arrival that Honeysuckle ever left the ship."

"Really?" I was surprised to hear that. She did not seem overly frightened by the outdoors on the times that she went out with me. At least not much more than the others.

"And Vanilla still has yet to step outside," Cinnamon added.

I hadn't given that much thought. Her work was in her lab, so of course she would remain within the safety of the ship. The more that we expand our compound though, the more we might just alienate her. That could seriously shift the balance of power toward Sage. I would need to address that.

"So, would you like to sleep in my bed again tonight?" I asked my favorite girl. We had yet to have sexual relations, but hugs and kisses were always welcome. I needed to keep things going in the right direction with her. Steady progress was my goal.

"I don't think so," she answered with an apologetic smile.

"Why not?"

Cinnamon slumped in her chair as she frowned. It was not something that I liked seeing. Had I done something to offend her? If so, I would need to fix it. Not only was I growing incredibly fond of her she would also be very instrumental to my future among the crew.

"I don't want to feel like I belong to you," she explained. "I'm just going to sleep in my own bed tonight."

"Well, I could sleep with you there if you want. With it being your room, it will be different."

"No, not really," she cracked a meager smile at my attempt.

My ego kicked in and fed words to my mouth that I didn't really want to say. Too many mistakes in my life had begun that way. "So, I'm going to have to spend the night with one of the other girls?"

"That's up to you," Cinnamon replied, stiffening a little at me going on the defense. "If you can get one of them to join you, go for it."

"You don't think I can..." I started. My ego took another jolt. "I don't know if you have heard, but..."

"Oh, I've heard plenty about your time with both Coffee and Honeysuckle," she cut me off. "Neither of them are shy about sharing details. But you should know that they don't plan to be on call for you, either. They had been depraved of sex for a while and came across as more eager than they intended, I believe. I don't know how it was in your time, Kash, but women these days don't physically need a penis induced orgasm all that often."

Initially that sounded like bad news. Then I gave it some thought. "Women in my time were kind of like that, too. But it varied quite a bit by individual. So, when not sex deprived, how often do you girls need some boom boom?"

"Boom boom?" she laughed. I was glad that I was able to lighten the mood after my blunder.

"Yeah, sexual penetration."

"Oh," she replied sheepishly. "I couldn't speak for the other ladies."

"Then just speak for yourself," I told her. When she hesitated to answer, I added, "I'm simply curious. As you know I am extremely interested in developing my relationship with you. I'm prepared to take it as slow as you need to go. This tidbit of information will help me in the future, if you don't mind telling me."

Cinnamon turned slightly in her chair. I got the impression that she might just leave without answering. I touched her arm and apologized. It shocked me when I did, because I had never been one to say that I was sorry unless it was absolutely necessary. Despite the perceived attack on my pride, I was concerned about her feelings.

"If you must know," Cinnamon said softly without turning to face me. "I've never had sex, Kash. I'm still a virgin."

When my hand slipped from her elbow she urgently stood up and went to her room. I might not be the smoothest romancer in the galaxy, but I knew not to follow her. I was going to have to make some big adjustments to my plan anyway. Maybe I should direct my primary attention to one of the other girls. If I wanted to be King of Dragon planet, I would need a strong queen. I was suddenly unsure that Cinnamon could be that for me.

CHAPTER FOUR:

I was certainly wary of my situation. Being alone outside was undoubtedly dangerous enough. Going out with a suspected murderer doubled the potential for a fatal experience. Add the murderer's closest friend and possible accomplice to the scene and the need for caution was an extreme understatement.

Sage had suggested that we take a look at the cliff situation from outside. Surprisingly, no one had done so previously. The logic she used to support who should go had plenty of merit. The three of us were the top ranking among the crew, especially regarding outdoor projects. We were also the most skilled in use of the weapons to minimize our hazard.

With just the two registered weapons, though, her choice for bearing them had me concerned. Sage took the energy rifle and assigned the bolt pistol to Strawberry. The latter was equipped with a sturdy black holster that I did not previously know about.

"You'll have your new sword," Sage justified her decision. "You have been quite impressive with it."

I assumed that the compliment was meant to appease me. But there was no denying that a sword was worthless against a gun at any range beyond a few feet. Was I supposed to be able to deflect bullets with it? Or balls of energy? Of course, I wasn't supposed to be expecting to defend myself against them.

No matter. I surprised them both when I met them at the exit with the new pistol from cargo that merely shot electricity. They knew of its existence and wrote it off as practically useless, just like I did. They had second thoughts when they spotted it in my hand.

The other hazard was the cliff itself. The ship's computer informed us that the immediate drop was nearly thirty meters. That was a hundred feet to me, and a slim chance of surviving if I were to slip off. Or be pushed.

Understandably, none of us were eager to get close to the edge. We didn't need to anyway. We could clearly see the situation from a safe distance. The front left corner of the ship was hanging over the cliff.

Instead of the bottom of the remaining portion of hull resting on solid ground, there was a shitload of destroyed vegetation directly beneath it. You would think that the weight of the ship would pancake it all. But red logs were wedged in there still nearly intact.

Some of the variance calculated by the ship's computer, regarding us slipping over the edge of the cliff, was adjusting each time a log split. Or pieces dropped over the edge. That explained the almost constant fluctuation in the calculation.

"What brilliant ideas do you have for this situation, Kash?" Sage placed one hand on her oversized hip as she gave me a serious look. It was hard not to be distracted by her extreme hourglass figure. Her t-shirt could barely contain her huge chest melons. Apparently, the unfastened uniform top stopped trying long ago. It was always left open when I saw her. I was quite sure that the previous men of the ship had no complaints about that fashion statement.

"I'm working on it," I replied.

Sage raised one eyebrow and tilted her head, obviously not expecting that reply. The situation did look hopeless. Strawberry could be seen behind her smiling. One thing that I liked about that girl was her sense of humor. And her flirty nature. So, two things. The strawberry shortcake look was a bit hit and miss for me. If only she wasn't so strongly aligned with my opposition.

"There are things that we could do to stabilize the situation," I told her. "But the work would be extremely dangerous. We'd have to use the loader bot..."

"No way!" Sage shook her head adamantly. "Those things are so experience. It would take more than the revenue from our entire cargo to buy a new one of those."

"At least a replacement can be bought," I told her. "If we have a crew member crushed by the weight of the ship, they are never coming back."

"That's a good point," Strawberry said as she walked up to join us.

"What about you?" Sage asked her friend. "Do you have any suggestions for improving our circumstances here?"

"I've got nothing," she replied immediately. "Unless Kash has some epiphany, I suggest that we continue with the plan of doing repairs while moving a bunch of our stuff outside. That seems like the best course of action to me."

We took some photos and videos of the scene beneath the hull so we wouldn't have to come back again. Strawberry got dangerously close to the edge trying to get the proper angle to see around a large red tree trunk. When she went to stand up her little boot slipped.

Strawberry's weight immediately shifted to compensate for one shoe not gripping. It caused her other foot to slide out from under her as well. What had appeared to be reasonably stable mossy ground turned out to have slick slimy mud just underneath.

I saw panic in Strawberry's eyes as her flat belly hit the ground and both her lower legs dangled over the edge. Her bubbled butt contributed too much weight to her lower half. She grabbed desperately for a handhold on the loose fern like growth to no avail. The slippery surface combined with the slight grade was attempting to send her over the edge.

I quickly released the grip on my electro pistol and dropped to my knees. Both hands flew forward to quickly grab the endangered redhead by two delicate wrists. She released the shredded ground cover from her fingers and put her full trust in me.

I stared into her eyes as I spread my knees wider for more stability. To her credit, the suddenly incredibly attractive woman did not scream for help. She fully understood her situation and knew that screaming would be a waste of energy. It could also possibly draw the attention of predators nearby. What I saw in her eyes was more than recognition of the physical hazard. She knew that I had some motivation to let her drop to her death.

As harsh as I could be sometimes, killing Strawberry at this point was beyond my limits. Added to that fact was her alluring damsel in distress appearance. My heart required that I did everything that I could to save her.

I had expected Sage to be right there with me, grabbing her friend before she could slide off the cliff. To my knowledge this was her closest friend and strongest supporter. I glanced back to see her sexy boots planted in the same exact spot that they had been before the incident.

There was no sense in calling for her help. She clearly wanted to see how this played out. Losing Strawberry would be catastrophic to her hold on the crew. However, if I went over the edge with her, it just might be worth it in her eyes. It was one thing to calculate and plot against others. Standing idly by as they dropped to their death was something completely different. Even with the rumor of what happened to the captain, I had clearly underestimated her. Sage could be a stone-cold killer.

I was determined to keep us both alive. However, if I couldn't, I knew that I would have to release my grip on the freckled ship systems officer to save myself. The question was, could I protect myself fast enough after I let go? Or would there be a boot in my back as soon as I did? Or a rifle shot to the back of my head execution style?

The girls would have a fit if there was evidence that Sage killed me in cold blood. If Strawberry died as well, there could be enough doubt to immobilize them. But were any of them really strong enough to stand up to her? Probably not.

I pulled my shoulders back first with my arms still extended. Strawberry's petite frame slid toward me a few inches. My right knee slipped, but not enough to cause a real concern just yet. Utilizing the full power of my biceps I slowly pulled my hands toward my chest, her arms coming with them. Again, she gained ground. A couple kicks at the ground placed her nearly in my arms. Actually, her face was closer to my crotch.

I fully expected a desperate bear hug. Or at least a madly appreciative embrace. Instead, she caught herself before her emotional state could push her that far.

"Thank you, Kash," Strawberry whispered. I saw the sincerity in her eyes, but her face had taken on a more serious and business-like appearance. Then I watched as she pulled her pistol from its holster.

Holy fuck! Did I just save this girl so that she could kill me in return? Was it some elaborate trick to catch me off guard and weaponless? That would explain why Sage did not get involved. But there was no safety net for Strawberry. She could have literally fallen to her death. Did she not mean for it to be that close?

I reached for my sword hanging from my waist. It was pinned under her left thigh. Her skin was warm and silky smooth, blocking any easy access to my life saving weapon. Before I could manage to get my fingers around the handle she spoke again.

"Don't," she whispered as she pulled her gun to my shoulder, keeping it close to her body.

If she was planning on killing me there was no reason to follow that order. I'd rather go down fighting than be executed in a vulnerable position. When I saw her head tilt to her right, along with her pistol, a saw a more fearful expression spread across her lovely, freckled face. She then looked past me at her leader, Sage.

"What are you doing with Kash's pistol," Strawberry asked her friend pointedly.

"Oh, Sweet Berry," Sage replied casually. But it sounded fake to me. "Don't be silly. I'm just holding it for him."

I turned to see Sage with her rifle in her right hand, pointed toward the ground still, but more like a forty-five-degree angle. If she pulled the trigger it might even hit my ass. In her left hand was the pistol. She held it by the handle at a similar tilt.

My fear about Sage's intention during our little expedition to the cliff had merit after all. Why else would Strawberry react the way that she did? She had to know that Sage would take an opportunity to kill me. Perhaps my coming to her aid in a life-threatening situation changed her mind about going through with some plan that they constructed together.

"Come," Sage told us as she took a couple steps backwards. "Both of you should get away from the edge."

Strawberry shifted to climb off of me. She had advanced upward to the point that she been straddling my lap, a position that I had suddenly become more receptive to with her, only in a completely different setting. As we stood, she pushed ahead of me to place her body between mine and her double weapon leader.

I had my hand around the hilt of my sword as I waited to see how things played out. I realized then that my new redhead friend was warning me not to draw my weapon and escalate the situation. Much shorter than me, I was able to watch over her shoulder as she stepped forward and reached for my pistol. Sage released it to her care with a smile that almost looked painful.

Without turning her back on the highest-ranking officer of the crew Strawberry handed me the nearly useless electro-pistol. I took it with my left hand as I studied the situation. Was there still going to be a shootout? Had Strawberry completely swapped sides?

"I think that we are done here," Strawberry said with a slow even tone. "Don't you, Sage?"

"Yes," our exaggerated hourglass figured leader replied in clear disappointment. "It appears as though you are correct. I believe that we have all that we need."

When Sage turned her back to us and walked inland from the cliff, we both watched for a few seconds. Once she cleared the corner and disappeared from view, Strawberry turned to me.

"Thank you for real, Kash," she said, just before she placed her bold red lips to my cheek. She lingered just a few inches from my face for a moment studying my eyes. Then, abruptly she turned and followed Sage back to the entrance to the ship. Not another word was spoken until we were back inside. Then Sage asked Strawberry to place all three firearms back in the weapons cabinet.

Sage sighed while looking at me as her friend followed her orders. Her disappointed look said, *what am I going to do with you?*

CHAPTER FIVE:

I informed my favorite three girls of what happened outside of the ship. If I had to assign a single emotion to each of them, I would say that Honeysuckle was angry, Cinnamon concerned, and Coffee scared.

"We have to do something now," Honeysuckle said to us with her fists clenched.

"With Strawberry wavering, this might be our best chance," Coffee added.

It was good to see their support for me growing each day. Once again Sage's backfired plan had worked to my advantage. Not only was I growing in favor among these three I also had a legitimate chance of pulling Sage's first officer over to my side.

I studied their faces for a moment. If Cinnamon would not be the best choice for my top woman in the future, which of these other two would? Coffee was not aggressive enough, I thought. Except when it came to sex. But according to Cinnamon that may have been a one-time thing from being depraved. Honeysuckle might be the better choice, but her wide range of emotions had me concerned. That's when I realized that the most suitable female on the ship to be at my side was without a doubt Strawberry.

The fiery redhead was devoted, determined, calm in a crisis, and exuded confidence at all times. But how would I make this happen? Would I lose support from these three if I made a strong move to recruit the woman? Honey would be pissed for sure. I still hadn't figured out what was going on between the two of them.

Before I could reply to Honeysuckle's statement that we needed to do something, Cinnamon spoke up. "Not yet," was all that she said.

The other two girls looked at her. At that moment I saw the respect that they had for my best friend. They each released a slow breath and nodded. They didn't even glance to me to see how I felt about things. The girls must be meeting and talking among themselves. That was not surprising. I just didn't realize that Cinnamon had become the unspoken leader of the group.

When it came to ship's rankings, Cinnamon was at the bottom with Honeysuckle. However, there was something about her personality that made the others want to follow her example, if not her lead. Possibly even more than they would follow mine. Remove sex from the equation and I might not have that strong of a hold on these girls.

Perhaps I was wrong about Cinnamon after all. Maybe she would make the perfect queen for me. The quiet type that only spoke when needed. The kind that everyone respected. I would just need to groom her better for the position. And bed her, too.

The truth of the matter was that I was not ready to launch a power play. Not anywhere near ready. The best thing for me to focus on was making steady gains, even if my momentum was slow.

Coffee reluctantly joined me for harvesting the drinking water from the mist trappers. We were getting more efficient at it each time. As we worked, she asked me to show her how big the new outdoor camp would be. I motioned and pointed as I explained but ended up placing marks in the dirt to show the large L shape from the middle of the right side of the ship to the middle of the rear. The effort even made me more excited about building it.

We sat our water containers at the corner of the spaceship while we planned how to position the crates from storage. Just as we were about to retrieve them, I heard the sound of a Wofur approaching.

I had the pistol and my sword. That gave me confidence that I could protect us but facing a charging wild animal was never a calm experience. I held my firearm ready as I waited for the beast to appear. It didn't take long before it rounded a large bush, focused on me with its snout down low. And it was huge. Nearly twice the size of the last one that I killed, and easily the biggest one that I had ever seen.

"Woah, buddy," I said to it, repeating its own sound. That might not be a good idea. Most animals were able to communicate with others of their kind even though all of their language sounded the same to us. For all I knew my imitation of the noise it made could be a derogatory remark toward its mother.

The bear like predator plodded slowly forward, then stopped at roughly thirty feet away. I was certain that I could fire a bolt into its head at that distance. And I was ready to do so until it stopped moving forward. When it glanced to my right, I caught the movement of another one out of the corner of my eye. Though not quite as big, it was closer as it pushed through some tall grass. I had been too distracted to notice the telltale signs of the yellow and green blades being split apart.

"Oh, fuck," Coffee said from right behind me. I had stepped in front of her the moment that I heard the first one coming. "Should we run?" she asked.

"No," I said calmly, for her benefit as well as mine. My heart was racing as much as when the blue dragons attacked me on top of the ship. "But it might be a good idea for you to take the pistol."

"No way," Coffee replied. "You could shoot them both before I'd even take aim. Do it."

The pair of Wofurs were edging forward as we talked. The big one was five feet closer. I knew it could be on me in a second if it charged. The other one was just a dozen feet away. I didn't have any more time to debate. Coffee was right. I needed to shoot.

I swiveled to the right and took aim quickly. The motion set them both off. Pop! my pistol sent a slug into the forehead of the smaller one. It was still three times the size of a German Shepherd. It instantly stopped in its tracks but did not fall.

Coffee screamed frantically from behind me. I rotated back to the larger beast as it launched itself into the air. The cone shaped snout split to reveal rows of sharp teeth. I fired my second shot, but not before my body reacted to the anticipated impact from the predator's attack. The bolt grazed its front left leg and had no impact on its trajectory.

I dodged out of the way of its freakish clawed hand, but the elbow struck my shoulder with so much weight that I was quickly thrown to the ground.

Coffee scurried to the nearest ladder embedded in the side of the ship and started to climb. The big Wofur hesitated as it tried to decide which one of us would be the easier meal. That moment allowed me to raise up on my hands and knees facing the thing. I glanced around looking for my pistol.

The alien bear was smarter than I could have imagined. It knew what I was looking for, and it found it before me, on the ground right in front of us. When it placed its stubby fingers on the weapon I freaked out. Was I really going to get shot by a wild animal?

Instead, it used its hand to swat the pistol a few feet farther away from me. As I debated about trying to retrieve it, I heard a thud directly behind me. The other Wofur had finally fallen over, but not before taking several more steps in my direction. Its angry snout dropped just inches from my boot.

My confusion gave the beast its golden opportunity to charge me again. I pulled my new sword from my belt and fumbled with the buttons. I managed to extend the blade, but it was still guarded when the Wofur ran its massive body into it, knocking it out of my hands.

Once again, I was able to dodge the front claws, but its left rear finger-foot struck my left hip. The continuous motion of its limb powered through my clothes and flesh to create three deep cuts halfway down my thigh. I screamed out in agony.

"Kash!" Coffee yelled at me. But she was simply panicking. It would have been a good time to retrieve the pistol and save my ass. Or call for the girls inside the ship to help us. Unfortunately, she was paralyzed as she hung from the ladder halfway up the side of the hull.

I managed to hold onto my weapon this time. My eyes were clenching shut from the pain, but I was able to find the right button to remove the blade guard. The next time the thing charged I swung the sharp edge wildly toward its head.

The Wofur apparently was less familiar with swords than it was firearms. It did not expect to take damage from my weapon. Why would it.? The last time that it made contact with it the blade it was still guarded. Its face didn't even have time to react to the injury as I managed to cut the fucker's whole head off. It dropped onto my chest and the rest of its body barely missed my legs, taking two more steps before its muscle memory failed it.

Rancid black blood rolled out of both the severed head and the neck to soil my shirt and the ground around me. I pushed the nasty thing off my chest as I tried to scramble away from it. Only my left leg wasn't working so well. I nearly passed out when I saw how bad the wound was. The cut might be as deep as the bone.

"Fuck!" I yelled.

Coffee was nearly to the bottom of the ladder before she stopped with a shocked expression, pointing beyond me. "Look out!" she screamed.

I struggled to turn my head far enough to see what she was pointing at. Was it another Wofur coming to seek revenge for its dead family members? No, the large shadow that blocked out the sun could only be that of a dragon.

"Oh shit!" I murmured as I reached for my weapon. It had somehow guarded and retracted when I scurried away from the Wofur carcass, perhaps to avoid cutting me. Then I heard the painfully slow dragon speech from above me.

"What is fuck?" it asked.

The snout of the huge green dragon descended toward me. If it intended to eat me, I would be unable to stop it. Fortunately, I recognized the face and the voice. Or at least I thought that I did. For all I knew all green dragons looked and sounded alike.

I released a heavy breath as I slid backwards to rest on my elbows. I stared up at what I hoped was my friend Gako. I didn't have the energy to answer his question.

"I know what shit is," he then said in his slow deep voice.

I started to laugh. But with the fear of being eaten subsiding, the pain returned in full force.

"You need the river water to heal," Gako told me. He must be referring to the murky green liquid that made me sleepy. And made my feet and legs all tingly. And gave the other men raging boners. As I was processing that information, he spoke again. "Your woman is useless."

"Hey!" Coffee took offense to the remark. It must have snapped her out of her panic, but she had climbed back up the ladder to the midway point. Surely, she had to know that she couldn't hide from a dragon up there.

"Only in a battle," I replied to the dragon. "She is great in other ways."

"Really?" Gako asked. I imagined invisible eyebrows raising as he pondered how good Coffee might be in bed. I started laughing again, but it was short lived due to the pain.

"This is Gako," I told my chocolate, tattooed female companion. "He's the one that helped me kill the blue dragon."

Gako raised his neck to look toward Coffee as she remained in the same place, clinging to the rungs of the ladder. I fully expected them to begin talking to each other. Instead, they just stared for a moment.

When the dragon turned his attention back toward me, he asked, "Are you going to eat that?"

He was of course referring to the dead wofurs. I had provided him with a like meal just yesterday. Considering that he also ate much of the blue dragon on the hull I was a bit surprised that he was the least bit hungry. It wasn't like he was doing much during the day. His daily routine seemed to comprise mostly of napping in the red tree. Of course, I had no idea what he was doing while I wasn't watching. Maybe he was having regular sex with a dozen female dragons.

"No," I replied. "Please, take them both. Get them out of here."

"I am not your cleaning servant," Gako said to me. Then he locked his massive jaw around the body of the headless alien bear. It had to weigh at least four hundred pounds. His neck muscles flexed as he lifted the dead animal a few inches off the ground.

When Gako turned to leave I was worried that his tail would swing around and knock the shit out of me. Fortunately, he curled it upward to avoid the contact as he hauled his meal to the base of his massive tree. My hopes that he would immediately return for the severed head were dashed when he plopped down and began eating.

"You need to get to medical immediately," Coffee yelled to get my attention as she approached. With fear of the dragon gone she was returning to my side.

My wound was certainly bloody. I realized then that the tiredness taking me over may have been due to the loss of blood.

"Fuck!" I screamed as I tried to put weight on my injured leg. Coffee's small frame was struggling to assist me to a standing position. Then I heard something pushing through the grass from the rear of the ship. "Grab the gun!" I told her.

She was hesitant to let me go. By the time that she spotted the discarded weapon on the ground we realized that it was not another wofur attacking. I saw red hair and the tip of the rifle barrel first as Strawberry rounded the corner of the craft. After clearing the area of threats, she slid under my right arm to help Coffee carry me back inside. My feet were dragging the ground by the time that we reached the entrance. I was passed out before the door closed behind us.

Groggily I awoke sometime later, completely naked, reclined on the lounge in the medical bay. One of Vanilla's hands was on my injured thigh, her knuckles resting against my scrotum as she scanned my healing wound with her device. It should also be noted that I had a raging hard-on.

CHAPTER SIX:

"Could you please not have an erection at this moment," Vanilla said once she realized that I had awakened. There was something more than awkwardness in her voice. Embarrassment?

"I didn't have much control over that," I mumbled as I checked my injury. The cuts were sealed up, but nasty pink lines remained. They looked like the beginning of a scab forming.

"Ah, yes," Vanilla replied as she tapped the screen a couple times with her thumb to bring up a different scan type. "I believe that you referred to it as morning wood. Are you always aroused when you wake up?"

"Especially if a gorgeous nurse is caught fondling my ball sack," I replied.

Vanilla pulled her hand away quickly with a shocked look on her face. Instead of looking defensive she had the appearance of someone that had been caught doing something that they shouldn't. "I was not fondling anything!"

I laughed as I checked out her angelic appearance. Just then the creamy brown shimmer flashed across the pale skin of her chest. Her uniform top was unfastened farther than I had ever seen it before, halfway down, revealing her ample cleavage. Her flowing brown hair of multiple shades shifted on its own, but never revealed the unique ears that were rumored to exist.

I reached down and grabbed my boner out of habit. It was super rock hard. Did she give me some kind of medicine that had such of an effect?

"I think that you must have been touching it," I told her in jest. "It is certainly ready for action."

"I... I...," Vanilla stuttered as she stepped back, ceasing her examination suddenly. "I may have had to move it out of the way a couple times," she then told me, averting her eyes.

It was funny to see her respond that way. She was usually so professional. I couldn't resist the urge to tease her some more.

I pretended like I was examining my penis for signs of tampering. "The head is a little wet," I lied to her. "Were you licking it?"

"What?" Vanilla's reaction said that maybe I had gone too far. She looked appalled. "No! I would never."

I bounced my balls in my other hand as I sat up on the lounger. I was acting as if I was weighing them. "My nuts seem kind of full. You must have been doing something naughty for a while as I was asleep."

"No!" she replied, looking more concerned than offended. "That can't be. I barely did anything!"

"Oh," I responded with exaggerated big eyes. "So, now you admit to playing with it. Tell me, Doc. What exactly did you do with my cock?"

Vanilla was flustered. Her anger was completely gone. She suddenly looked like she might just break down and cry. I had gone too far. I needed to apologize.

"Vanilla..." I started.

"I'm sorry, Kash," she then said, staring at the floor. "I did touch it more than was necessary. It is a gross violation of your privacy. Please don't tell the others. I would be so embarrassed if the girls found out. I need their respect to do my job properly."

"Oh, okay," I told her. I was not expecting a confession. I hadn't really suspected that she had done anything wrong. But now that I knew, I wanted to hear more. "Just tell me what exactly happened."

"Well," she explained, only glancing at my face periodically. Her attention had shifted from the floor to my crotch where I still had both hands in position but motionless. "It was not hard yet, but it was growing when I moved it out of the way to treat your wound. As the muscle firmed up, your penis kind of flopped back over to the wounded thigh. I believe that it may have a natural tendency to lean that way."

It was true. I had a beautiful penis, but it did not hang perfectly straight. I could easily visualize it returning to my left thigh as it enlarged. I didn't particularly care for someone pointing out that flaw, though.

"The next time I moved it," Vanilla continued without my urging. "I studied it more closely, out of personal interest, not professional. The organ reacted steadily to my touch. Once I realized that an erection would actually keep it out of the way, I kind of played with it a little."

What the fuck? I was certainly not offended. Instead, I was delighted that my joking nature had me stumble into such unexpected admission of guilt.

"Played with it how?" I asked, trying hard to act more concerned than excited.

"Well, I..." she started to say as she made a stroking motion with her empty hand.

"No," I cut her off. I pulled my own hands away from my goods. "Show me."

"No, Kash," Vanilla shook her head. But she didn't seem to be totally committed to rejecting the idea. Or maybe I was just hoping that was the case. "That would be inappropriate."

"You have already been inappropriate," I told her softly, not wanting to be pushing the wrong button. "I promise not to tell anyone what you have done, but for my peace of mind I just need to see what you did. Then we can be done with it."

I saw her reluctance, then mere hesitation, but she did not refuse. I waited until finally she reached forward to grab my boner. Her hand wrapped around the upper half with her forefinger and thumb encasing the edge of the head. Between the sensation and the sight, I felt a surge in my testicles.

Vanilla then began stroking my cock as I watched in amazement. When she sat down her medical scanning device to join in with the second hand I was delighted. Even more so when she gently massaged my balls from the bottom.

"I did this for maybe a whole minute, Kash," she whispered as she looked me in the eye. I could finally see an ornery side of her personality trying to get out. "I'm very sorry," she whispered with a thin smile as she continued to work my genitalia.

"Could you please continue for another minute?" I asked.

I knew my request was improper. I fully expected a rejection and her full return to a professional demeanor. She did not reply. Nor did she stop.

I ogled her fine body and beautiful face as she continued at a slow but effective pace. When I reached for her breast, she pulled her shoulder back and told me no. I waited a moment then tried again, this time just running one finger between her impressive cleavage. Luckily, she accepted it.

Then I reached for the side of her face. She stopped stroking me suddenly and informed me that she wasn't going to suck me. Apparently, she thought that I was going to grab her by the back the head and force her mouth onto me.

"No," I whispered. "I just want to see your ear."

"Oh," she responded, returning to her regular handjob rhythm. She then tilted her head to the side and her hair gracefully flowed backwards out of the way, as if she willed it to do so.

Her ear was just as Honey had described it. Small, delicate, pulled up against her skull only a little more than an average person. And the top was pointed. Not sharp like an arrowhead. It rounded smoothly at the tip with skin that perfectly matched the rest of her body. It even shimmered as the wave of brown moved across her skin.

She turned her head toward me and leaned forward allowing me to touch it. I carefully caressed every line of her ear, then started again. I never had an ear fetish. I wasn't even sure if that was a real thing. But Vanilla's ear was easily the most attractive that I had ever seen. I was mesmerized by it.

When I started grunting and my hips began their tiny little convulsions, she knew that I was getting close to climaxing. I thought that would be the end of the show. She would stop short kind of like Sage did that time in her room. I had gotten much more out of this experience than I had expected, so I was mentally prepared to deal with that scenario. Instead, she reached for a bedpan.

Holding the basin in front of me she squeezed tighter and quickened her pace. She was urgently rewarded with several spurts of my semen striking the inside of the pan. Her jaw dropped open as she watched. I was concentrating on not letting my orgasm force my eyes closed. I knew that I would want to replay this scene in my head over and over again.

She released her grip on the shaft to squeeze the tip of the head with her thumb and finger, taking the rest of what I had to offer into the palm of her hand. Then she went about the process of cleaning up as I worked to control my breathing.

"We shall not speak of this to anyone, correct?" she asked.

"Of course," I told her. Maybe keeping this secret could improve my chances of getting more sexual activity with her in the future. Or I could use it as leverage when I was ready to make a move on Sage. Either way, I had no intention of telling the others.

"And you forgive me?" she asked, looking me in the eye.

"For what?" I asked. I should be thanking her after the amazing handjob. Why would she need forgiveness?

"For touching you in your sleep, of course," she answered with a smile. "I promise never to do it again."

"Oh," I said. "Actually, I would love for you to do it again some time."

Vanilla laughed, but a moment later she was back to being my doctor. She placed a small cloth over my penis that looked like it was ready for a nap. "Let's cover that thing up while we finish healing your leg."

I relaxed as a song came to mind. One of my perverted versions:
I've got so much spunky,
porn stars envy me.
When it's cold outside

my balls get shrivel and retreat.
I guess, you say,
Who can make me feel this way?
Vanilla…Doctor Vanilla!

CHAPTER SEVEN:

Vanilla placed me on light duty for a couple days. Actually, she said no work for the first day, and slowly increasing my workload over the next three days. My injury had been healed medically, but it would take a few days for my thigh muscle to recover.

I had no intention of following her instructions to the letter. But I did allow myself to sleep in the next morning. After breakfast I read my messages and studied some training courses on the ship's engine design. I was no longer clueless about how the ship was powered, but I was still a bit bewildered. It was kind of like skipping algebra and going straight to calculus. The math worked, but my understanding was very limited.

I was itching to do something after just two hours. Funny that. I spent months in a prison cell with nothing to do. Now I can't go a whole day without getting something accomplished.

I did a dozen squats to test my leg. My hot doctor, the pointed eared queen of handjobs, was very clear not to do any exercise for the thigh until the next day. But I was hard-headed. Nothing snapped inside my thigh, but a pain resonated from deep within to tell me to stop.

Wincing and limping when no one was looking, I hobbled down into the lower level. The cargo section was empty of people, but I could hear Honeysuckle and Cinnamon conversing in the engine room. I debated on joining them, but something called me to the forward cargo section instead. I hadn't spoken to Teddy recently. Something told me that he'd be up for a chat.

I coded the central cargo hold and shut the door behind me. I wasn't sure why. Maybe I didn't want anyone to know where I was. Of course, they could always find me. Cameras weren't even needed. The ship's computer tracked all official crew members. I didn't get the data chip behind the ear yet but wearing the communicator bracelet was enough.

I did the same with the forward hold door. I was surprised to see Teddy standing in his cage, hands on the bars, facing me as I entered. Normally he was so bored that he could hardly be bothered to notice who walked in. The girls claimed that he was getting even grumpier than before.

"How are you feeling, Kash?" Teddy asked me in that sad monotone voice of his. Had he been informed of my injury? He usually didn't talk to the females, but that didn't mean that one of them didn't inform him when they came to feed him.

"I'm okay," I answered, thrown off a bit by the feeling that he had somehow lured me in to see him.

"You are favoring one leg," he then said.

"I was attacked by a beast native to this planet."

"A dragon?" he asked. It was actually a little hard to tell when he was asking a question because he lacked the rise in inflection at the end of the sentence. It was also difficult to know if something you said surprised him for the same reason.

"No, something smaller," I told him. "It is dead now."

"It would almost have to be if you survived. Did you use your new sword?"

"Yes, as a matter of fact I did. How did you know?"

"I didn't," Teddy responded as he turned and walked to the back of the cage and sat down.

I didn't like how this conversation was going. How was an alien trapped in a cage getting the upper hand on me? Yet still, I was intrigued. I decided to mimic his actions and casually sit down somewhere. I didn't want to put my back against the cage of one of the other animals, so I leaned against the cube with all the food.

On the top right corner of each cage was a keypad. I would have expected technology to have advanced beyond such a security measure, but when it came down to it, there were only two options for opening anything locked. A key or a code. A key could easily change hands. A code would have to be extracted from someone.

"Eight-six-nine-alpha-gamma-nine-six-two-alpha-nine," Teddy told me.

"Excuse me?"

"The code to my cage."

"If you knew the code, why haven't you used it?" I asked. Again, I felt like I was being led through this conversation.

"Then what?" he asked.

I thought about what I might do in his situation if I knew the code to release me from my close confines. Would I open it just to walk around the slightly larger forward cargo hold? Other than stretching my legs that wouldn't do much good. Teddy's legs were short, so that would be even less of an incentive.

No, I would definitely wait for an opportune time to release myself. A chance when I could escape the ship and achieve true freedom. Of course, if the ship were stranded on an alien planet, that could be an unbelievably bad long-term plan. I'd have to wait until the ship was repaired and we arrived at some new more desirable location.

With the ship on the edge of a cliff, though, that might never happen. Anything alive as the vessel dropped a hundred feet would probably die. So, the code did me no good really, unless a small percentage plan worked itself out.

It had to totally suck to sit and wait for such an opportunity. Oh wait, that was what happened to me. I was on death row waiting for execution when this mission of pushing me through a mysterious portal presented itself.

I got lucky. I knew that already but studying Teddy's situation made it even more clear.

Without another word said I stood up and keyed in the code that he told me. Sure enough, five of the bars broke in the middle and retreated in a telescopic fashion. There was more than enough room for Teddy to exit his cell.

I returned to my spot and sat back down. I was shocked that Teddy didn't immediately seize the opportunity to exit. That in itself told me that the tables had turned. I chose to release him of my own free will. I was not coerced. The question was how would he respond? His lack of action suggested that he did not expect me to do that.

I waited for a couple minutes, refusing to move or speak next. It was like a sales tactic, my father told me. Present the offer and wait. The next person to react loses. That pretty much described how salespeople viewed their customers. Opponents to be dominated. The decision to make a purchase meant that they lost, and the salesman won. That was a sad way to look at things, I always thought.

Finally, Teddy spoke from his seated position deep in his cage. "What happened to the other males?"

"Dead," was all I said. Never say more than you had to in a negotiation. Wait, was this a negotiation? Or was I simply so bored in my injured state that everything had become a game?

"I realize that," Teddy replied as he got up using his oversized arms to propel himself forward like an ape. I sat calmly as he exited his cage to sit in the middle of the floor. "How did they die?"

"Dragons," I answered after releasing a slow breath. I had my sword on my belt should Teddy try anything, but still, releasing a caged animal had its risks. Only I didn't really look at Teddy as an animal. Nor should anyone else, I surmised.

"Who's in charge?" he asked. There was no change in the expression of his fuzzy orange face on his triangular head. If there was any telltale to his emotional state in his tiny mouth, I was missing it.

"Sage," I replied without considering whether it was a bad idea to clue him in on the politics of our crew. "For now."

Teddy nodded. "I haven't met her yet. But I've picked up on some negative vibes from the others."

"Have you met Strawberry or Vanilla?"

"No, but they sound delicious," Teddy replied. Then he coughed. It took me a moment to realize that it was laughter instead. His mouth took on more of a squarish shape and the sound barked out. "Did you not like my joke?"

I then laughed genuinely. It was funny, after I realized that it was a joke.

"I may have spotted one of them before. I'm assuming Strawberry has red hair."

"Yes."

"Okay, I've seen her, but not Sage or Vanilla. Are they both your enemies?"

"Not Vanilla," I responded quickly. Then I got the feeling that I just revealed too much. It was a weird sensation in the back of my brain.

"Oh, you have a romantic interest in that one also," Teddy said. "How many of these women do you need to have sex with?"

I chuckled at the question. Then, after seeing that he was waiting for a response, I replied, "All of them. Except maybe Sage. I mean, I would love to tap that fat ass of hers, but she would need to be bound and gagged, I'd think. I wouldn't trust her in a normal sexual scenario."

Teddy nodded then said, "You know what I like about you, Kash? I learn more about the human language and method of thinking each time that we talk."

"So, what now?" I asked. "When I leave this room will you go back in your cage?"

"What choice do I have?"

None. I knew that, but I wasn't totally convinced that he did.

"You realize that we are stranded on some god forsaken planet where everything wants to kill us."

"So, I'm told."

"What would you do if I set you free?" I had asked that question before and he declined to respond. Now that he was at least out of the cage I thought that it was worth asking again.

"Why would you free me?" Teddy asked. "Considering the circumstances, what would you have to gain?"

Damn this was a sharp minded alien teddy bear. Then it clicked. How things could possibly work out for me. I had been focusing so much on which women would help me gain power. Yet, here I was the only human to have a dragon and an alien koala monkey bear as friends.

"If I give you a measured amount of freedom in exchange for your allegiance, is that something that you would be interested in?"

Teddy stared at me emotionless. Of course, that was his go to look for pretty much anything that happened. Then he said, "I believe the correct answer for you, Kash, is *hell fucking yeah*."

CHAPTER EIGHT:

"Oh, my stars," Cinnamon said when she entered the forward cargo hold. I had called her to join me there, not revealing why. She was shocked to see Teddy out of his cage. To her credit she did not scream out or retreat in fear. My presence and calm manner no doubt contributed to her reaction.

"How did...?" she began to ask glancing between us. "Never mind. What is the plan here?"

"The plan?" I asked.

"Yes, you called me in here for a reason," Cinnamon replied. "I'm assuming that you need my expertise, or you are looking for support in some new plan that involves the Pithynos being allowed some freedom."

She seemed to be in a bad mood. I was tempted to ask why, but that would just get us off subject. My best tactic would be to say something to get her to cool down before moving forward.

"Can't it just be because you are my best friend?"

Cinnamon took and released a deep breath then showed me a tired smile. "I'm sorry, Kash." Then she walked up to me and put her arms around my waist. Closing her eyes, she rested her head against my chest.

I wrapped my arms around her shoulders and kissed her on the top of the head, pausing briefly to breathe in her sweet scent.

"Love you, Cinny," I whispered. It was the first time that I had said those words and I chose to do so in a casual atmosphere for my own protection.

When she pulled back and looked me in the eyes, I thought that she just might tell me that she loves me, too.

"So, you say," she replied instead. "Now I'm definitely getting the impression that you need something from me."

I chose not to respond to the friendly accusation. Leaving one arm around her as she turned to face Teddy, I was happy to find him sitting in the same spot. Cinnamon had not bothered to close the door when she entered. I took his decision to not try and make a break for it an exceptionally good sign.

"Teddy," I said to him, emphasizing for Cinnamon's benefit that he had a name. There was no reason to continue calling him the Pithynos. "I need you to respect Cinnamon as you would me."

"He respects you, does he?" she asked me.

"We have a new arrangement," I explained. Then turning my attention back to Teddy, I said, "Can you do that?"

Teddy stared at Cinnamon for longer than was comfortable. I was beginning to think that maybe this was a bad idea.

"I will try," he finally responded.

"There is no try," I told him, quoting a remarkably similar sized fictional science fiction character. "Only do."

Blank stares from both of them. They obviously had not seen the movie.

"Follow her instructions and don't do anything that could cause her harm. Agreed?"

Teddy nodded and said that he agreed.

"What kind of instructions would I be giving him?" Cinnamon asked. "You don't plan to let him out of this room do you? Sage would have a serious fit. As would Vanilla."

"Why Vanilla?" I asked without giving it much thought.

"She's the ship's doctor, of course. There is a completely different protocol for a passenger than cargo. He would need a thorough examination."

"Will I enjoy the examination as much as Kash did his?" Teddy asked.

Cinnamon gave me a shocked and questioning look. I returned it. I never told Teddy anything about my private time with the gorgeous doctor. He just seemed to have a way of picking up on things better than most people. Vibes is what he called the clues that he studied. It was a term from my time that he must have learned from me.

"It doesn't matter, you little pervert," Cinnamon told Teddy. The words were harsher than her tone, but I wasn't sure how Teddy would respond. I was glad that he didn't go ape shit. "Sage will never allow it. To her, you are a precious piece of cargo."

"To be sold to the highest bidder," Teddy added.

"Maybe," she answered.

"Cinny," I said as I squeezed her shoulder. "He's not some..."

"I didn't say that I saw it that way. Only how Sage will see it. It's only her viewpoint that matters since she is in charge."

"For now," Teddy mumbled.

The conversation between the three of us wasn't going anything like I had pictured it. But it was surprisingly enjoyable just the same. And informative.

Cinnamon stared at him in shock. "What have you been saying to him, Kash?"

"Nothing," I answered defensively. "He's just very attentive."

During the pause in the conversation that followed I noticed for the first time that the other two animals were paying close attention, sitting calmly just inside the bars of their cage. Perhaps they were expecting to be released as well.

Finally, Cinnamon asked me again what my plan was. The truth was that I hadn't fully thought it through. I wanted her valuable input. And, in a way, I just got it.

"I want him free to roam the ship," I told her. "Eventually. But we'll need to take baby steps."

"Is that some sort of joke about the size of my legs?" Teddy asked. I laughed but did not respond verbally. I would need to figure out his sense of humor as we moved forward.

"Before he is allowed up top," I told Cinnamon. "He'll need to be cleared by Vanilla. We'll sneak him into her exam room and get her approval before facing Sage. Maybe, eventually, he'll be allowed outside."

"I don't think this will go the way that you think it will," Cinnamon replied. "But I'll go along with it as far as I can. Do you plan to release the other two animals, too?"

"What?" I asked. "No, of course not. Teddy is not an animal obviously. It is not the same."

"It will be to Sage, and more of the others than you might think," she told me.

"The big difference is that I can't have a conversation with the Tigritari or the Savrad," I explained.

Cinnamon nodded, but I could clearly see that she had serious doubts about this plan of mine. If I hadn't already made something like a promise to Teddy, I would seriously consider scrapping the idea for a while. I wouldn't want to let him go over the cliff with the ship, though.

Then Teddy said something that changed my mind completely. I had just said that I couldn't have a conversation with the other two animals.

"But I can," Teddy revealed.

If I could talk to the animals, I began singing in my head. Then I realized that I didn't remember any other lyrics for the song. Or any sexual references that could be substituted.

CHAPTER NINE:

"How long was the specific course to teach you how to repair that regulator?" I asked Honeysuckle. I had been studying general information about the ship's components for a couple days. Some of it made sense. Some of it I was still trying to grasp. One thing that I did learn was that every part of the ship was designed as simple as possible for durability and easy repair.

"Umm, I don't know," Honeysuckle replied from her kneeling position in front of the open panel. I had been watching her work, waiting for instructions on how I could help. "Maybe a couple hours?"

She was barefoot again, which seemed like a bad idea in a workspace such as the engine room. Her skinny green feet looked like an alien presence on the white tile floor. The clean appearance of the floor helped a mechanic find tools and parts when they dropped them, I was told.

Her uniform pants clung tightly to her perfect girlish ass, never revealing her butt crack despite her position. The top performed the same way. Her white hair was pulled back and clamped in place by a dark green comb that fit the shape of the back of her head. It was practical yet incredibly attractive at the same time. I was surprised that she didn't wear it more often.

"Why do you ask?"

I stopped ogling her sexy body and replied, "I was thinking that maybe each of us could learn some of the simpler repairs to take the workload off of you."

Honey stopped what she was doing and looked up at me like I had just said the most peculiar thing. "But… I'm the mechanic," she said.

"Yes, that is true. And you'll still be the mechanic long after we tackle these repairs."

"Tackle?"

"Of all the things that need done to make the ship flight ready," I said to her. "What percentage currently must be done by you?"

"Eighty?"

I had figured as much. That had the rest of the crew sitting around and waiting or piddling with non-essential projects. "And if the rest of us studied specific units, how many days training would it require for us to get your share down below fifty percent?"

Honeysuckle tilted her head back and forth as she calculated. I had a friend in high school that used to do the same thing. She was a natural blonde, though. I had no idea what Honey's original hair color was. "Two or three days."

"If we could cut your workload in half, how much time would that save us?"

She did that thing with her head again, this time sliding her the tip of her tongue out of the corner of her little mouth. With her head right about the height of my crotch I quickly lost focus until she finally answered.

"Maybe as much as two weeks."

I smiled big as I raised my hands to the side and said, "Then why don't we do that?"

She squinted at me and gave a crooked smile like she thought I was being silly. "Because I'm the mechanic. Why would the others want to learn something that is not their job?"

"To get off this planet faster," I replied like it was a no brainer. "If we could take off a week earlier just by you learning how to control the loader, would you do it?"

"Cinnamon's job?"

"Just the loader control," I told her. "This is a hypothetical question."

After few seconds she nodded and agreed that she would, assuming that she didn't already have enough work of her own. I told her that we should address that scenario with the others. Maybe just take volunteers to learn specific repair jobs.

"I don't understand how all this stuff got damaged in the crash," I changed the subject. The worklist to get the ship able to fly had a hundred small repairs along with the big ones. Was there some kind of domino effect? "It seems like some of these things are not related."

"You are right," Honeysuckle whispered to me like it was a delicate subject. "Some of the damage was caused before we crashed."

"By the weird atmosphere that blocks our communication?"

"Maybe," Honey replied. "Perhaps some of it."

"Well," I gestured for her to continue. "How did the other stuff get broken?"

Honey rose up to a standing position, placing her eyes right about the same level as my mouth. The white circles with dark green borders were freakish and yet still quite lovely. Again, I was quickly distracted. If it weren't for the tools in her hands, I could be led to believe that she wanted to be held in my arms. Kissed. Maybe even fondled.

"I believe that one component was sabotaged," she explained, leaning even closer to my face. The tilt toward me provided an enticing glimpse of her perfect green hooters. I felt my bottom lip drop uncontrollably due to her proximity. Hopefully, I wouldn't slobber. "That contributed to the failure of at least three other units. Together, they caused the crash."

"Wow," I replied in shock. That news got my attention. "One of you caused the crash on purpose?"

She nodded slowly while maintaining eye contact.

"Who?"

"I don't know."

"Have you shared this with Sage?" I asked. She didn't appear as though she recently had come to this conclusion. It would only be natural to inform the leader about this conspiracy theory. Only this was the first time that I caught wind of it.

"No," she answered, furrowing her brow. "I don't want to end up like the Captain."

Huh. Did that mean that Honeysuckle suspected that Sage was the saboteur? I was about to ask for more information when she sat the tools on a workbench and walked past me toward the doorway to the rest of the ship. Considering the topic for discussion I was curious what she was up to. Should I follow?

"Where are you going?" I asked.

"I have to pee."

I stood there bewildered as I watched her leave the room, quickening her pace like maybe she had been holding off emptying her bladder for too long. Who would want to crash the ship? Nobody, I would think. At least not anybody on the ship. They could have died from the impact. Why would one of the crew risk their own death?

Maybe, though, the sabotage wasn't intended to cause a crash. Perhaps the responsible person just wanted to force a landing. But why? What was to be gained by landing on this planet?

If the captain wanted to capture more animals to sell, he would simply have given the order to land. Forcing the ship down this way must have been done by someone that wasn't in command. And wanted their motives hidden. What else would be advantageous?

If someone in this crew did make this happen, they would have continued with their plan after crashing, I would think. What has been accomplished during their stay here?

The death of the captain and the pilot!

Sage probably forced the ship down so she could kill them both and take over as the next highest in command. I had heard the rumors about the sexually fueled anger that her and Strawberry had for the two previous men of the ship. That made me wonder if maybe Strawberry was in on it, too.

Hell, if I was Honeysuckle, I wouldn't have told Sage either. But would I keep it entirely to myself? If neither I nor my friends were at risk of being killed, maybe the best course of action would be to just let it alone. Repair the ship, take off, then quit the crew once I reached a secure location like a space station. Was that her plan before I brought up the subject?

Maybe they all knew about this conspiracy! As an outsider I just wasn't told about it. That made sense. They could have just gone about their business if it hadn't been for the unstable cliff that the ship rested on. Certainly, Sage hadn't expected them to be here so long, and need to find clean drinking water.

The whole story was starting to come together in my mind. Only Honeysuckle acted like this was a secret between her and me. If my power of deduction wasn't failing me, the secret was *only* from me.

Some of them were against allowing me on board. That could be for a variety of reasons. Others were for it. Again, there could be several factors there. Like sex. Were Honey and Coffee just horny? Hell, every one of them had already touched my cock except Cinnamon and Strawberry. And I anticipated that they too would join that list shortly.

I knew that it was weird to land my ass in such an incredible situation. Lucky, I told myself. Very, very lucky. But maybe my luck would soon run out.

Sage had already attempted my death a couple times, I believed. Was she the only one in on it? Were some pretending to be my friends just to set me up?

Honeysuckle revealing this secret to me could be an awfully bad thing. Did she just fuck me? Is that why she just padded away so quickly? Was she in a hurry to go somewhere other than the toilet?

I removed the sword from my belt and extended the blade. My finger hovered over the button to retract the guard. Would someone be coming for me soon? Is this where I will finally die?

I thought back to my conversation with Honeysuckle just a moment ago, looking for clues. I realized then that I was the one that led the discussion. She had no previous plan to reveal the sabotage to me.

When she just ran away, was it to inform the others of what she had done? If so, would they rush down here to kill me? Probably not.

I retracted the sword blade and placed the hilt back on my hip. I could always draw it again if I was wrong. I felt like I had inadvertently stepped into the rabbit hole that led to a whole new world of thinking. Again! First the portal to an alien world. Then learning that I had been transported to the future. And now, once again, finding out that things are not what I had assumed.

I heard footsteps coming down the stairs. I almost reach for my sword again, but it was clearly naked feet making the noise. Honeysuckle. I listened closely for someone following her. There was no indication that there was.

"Is everything okay?" Honeysuckle asked me when she returned back inside the engine room. I could only imagine the look on my face matching the wide range of thoughts running through my head.

I told her that I was fine, and she showed no sign of going on the alert. Perhaps she was not plotting against me after all. But the seed of doubt had been firmly established in my mind.

I continued thinking about it as I hovered by Honeysuckle while she finished the repair on the malfunctioning regulator. I honestly believed that some of the girls did not want me to die. At least not yet. But how much could I truly count on them?

I might just be paranoid. But I'd rather be overly cautious than end up dead. That would suck big time to survive my trip through the portal to another world, not get eaten by dragons, just to be slayed by conniving beautiful women. I needed to start working some other options.

CHAPTER TEN:

"I think that it is a great idea," Honeysuckle told the group. Every member had gathered together in the galley for a meeting. Even Vanilla was present. There were a few items on the agenda, but Sage had told me to go first. I wasn't sure if she was being agreeable or tactical.

"Well, of course you do," Sage replied. "It would be your workload that others will be doing for you."

"I'll do it," Cinnamon said next. It was perfect timing to distract from Sage's reaction. I figured that I could count on her to support the idea. But with recent developments I decided to evaluate every reaction for possible motivations. I was determined not to be caught off guard by fake friends.

Sage stared at Cinnamon for a moment as she formed words in her mind. She knew this was an important meeting for alliances among the crew. Before she could chastise Cinnamon for her announcement, Strawberry spoke up.

"I'd like to do some, too," she said, only glancing toward Sage briefly. "Anything that helps us get off this planet faster is a good idea."

Sage turned toward her second in command, struggling to control her shock. She looked betrayed. That was the great thing about not revealing your ideas before presenting them to the group. They couldn't plan a unified reaction.

"I'm in," Coffee joined the movement. "I just don't want to do any repairs outside."

"Kash and I will help Honey with the outdoor repairs," Cinnamon announced. "We'll be accustomed to working out there since we plan to build a base with our cargo cubes."

Sage was still trying to figure out how to twist this event to her advantage when Vanilla finally spoke up. Typically, she sat there quietly until a topic touched on her expertise. Such as edible food from the planet, air quality, and the like.

"I don't think that I'll be worth much with this endeavor," Vanilla said in her typical dignified manner. "I have no experience with mechanical operations."

"I'm sure that you can be a big help," I told the lovely doctor. "You are smart enough to learn anything, and you are very good with your hands."

The last comment reaped a sly smile from her, but then it quickly turned to a look of concern. The fact that no one else said a word afterwards indicated that I might have worded things wrong. Looking at the faces of the other women confirmed that they were all wondering what I meant.

"She's a doctor," I explained, trying not to give anything away. Vanilla's facial reaction certainly was not helping. "Doctors are notoriously good with their hands. I bet there are some repairs that require patience and a delicate touch."

"A delicate touch?" Strawberry asked with a sideways smile. Her sexual teasing was an admirable quality, one that drew me to her, but it wasn't working to my favor at the moment.

"Yes," Vanilla then said, recovering from her embarrassment and following my lead. "I believe I could do some things to help. I have more spare time than some of you."

It worked. Everyone began nodding their agreement like the motion had been approved. Everybody except Sage. It took her another moment to collect her thoughts before announcing that everyone could take on a repair assignment that otherwise would have been the mechanic's job. As long as it didn't interfere with their regular duties. Honeysuckle would have to assign something to each person based on their skill set.

"Does that include you?" Honey asked.

Everyone froze. Her question sounded too much like a challenge, especially given Sage's personality. Our paralyzed reaction only made it seem more so.

"Watch yourself, young lady," Sage said with the appearance of an offended queen.

"Sorry," Honey replied with a respectful dip of her head. "I just wanted to know whether to add you to my list of people that need assignments. That's all."

Sage calmed herself down and glanced toward Strawberry first. Perhaps she expected some support from her best supporter. Next, she looked at me, wondering whether I was going to use the opportunity to usurp her authority.

"I will come to you," Sage finally answered Honeysuckle. "When I am ready to help with the repairs."

Our two-hundred-foot-long home had not shifted much recently, but the chance of it slipping over the cliff had increased to over ten percent. Honeysuckle suggested completing the minimum number of repairs to fire up the engines so we could move the ship farther from the edge. Unfortunately, I had to agree with Sage on Strawberry that it was a bad idea. We were the three that saw firsthand what a precarious situation that we were in.

"I don't know everything about how your propulsion system works," I told them. "But I'd think that any vibrations made by the ship could cause the edge that we are resting on to collapse. We might fall over before we take flight."

"Well, we are going to have to lift off eventually," Cinnamon reminded us. "What makes the difference?"

"That's a good point," Sage replied, almost begrudgingly. "I think that we might need a slight adjustment to our plans."

She was evidently inviting suggestions, but most of the girls just stared at her. I took the opportunity to give it some thought. My heavy thinking face drew Strawberry's attention.

"Kash, do you have a suggestion?" she asked.

"Maybe," I responded, still working out details in my head. "How precise will the movement of the ship be if we do try to nudge it away from the cliff?"

"Very," Strawberry replied. "We'll program the details into the ship's computer, and it will perform the maneuver. In some ways it will be like docking to a station. There will be no chance of human error. However, we'll need to double check all vital systems to avoid mechanical error. What are you thinking?"

"How about we unload as much stuff as we can from the ship and stack it about a hundred feet away, over by the closest big red tree where Gako sleeps. We'll have to move our mist harvesters, too. That will lighten the ship to improve our balance. Then, instead of lifting off, we could program the thrusters to push us sideways at least fifty feet. Far enough that we don't have to worry about sliding over the edge while we finish our repairs."

"Yes!" Honeysuckle said excitedly. "Using only the lateral thrusters instead of trying to raise the ship off the ground should minimize the vibrations that could affect the stability of the cliff. The bottom hull can handle it, and the repairs required to make that happen are minimal. I just need to redo the list with new priorities."

"Excellent!" Strawberry responded. "We'll do that!'

Of course, it wasn't her decision. Just because she considered it the obvious solution didn't mean that Sage would approve. The leader needed a moment to consider what the shift would mean to her ulterior plan. Strawberry faced her, as we all did, and waited patiently. "What do you think?" she asked with a respectful tone.

Eventually our highest-ranking officer approved with a nod.

"I have a question," Coffee informed us. "Sage is taking over as captain obviously, while still handling navigation. But who is going to take over as pilot? Koradd and King were the only ones trained to fly our ship manually."

Apparently, no one had considered that point before. I had, but I was waiting until I had gained more knowledge before suggesting myself as the replacement. If it were me, I wouldn't want some stray homeless guy to be given the helm.

"Isn't it obvious," Strawberry said as she rested her delicate hand on my shoulder. She turned to me and smiled. "Kash should be the new pilot. We all have jobs to do on the ship after we leave this planet except him. It makes more sense to have him learn how to pilot instead of one of us."

"That's true," Cinnamon replied. The rest murmured their agreement. Even Sage.

"Kash," our leader addressed me. "You will have a lot to learn in a short amount of time. It will eat up all of your spare time and prevent you from having too many side projects. What do you think? Are you up for it?"

I wanted to consider all the possible implications of accepting the position, especially with the required time commitment. I might lose as much ground while studying as I would gain by becoming the new pilot. But there was really only one possible answer to give. And I was eager to give it.

"Yes," I answered. But I wanted to show my willingness to do new things that made me more valuable than others. "Of course, I'll do it. Whatever is needed to make us the best crew possible. I'll do what it takes."

CHAPTER ELEVEN:

I ventured outside with my first dirty girl, Cinnamon. She was caked up with Vanilla's scent blocking mud substitute. I personally had reduced the amount that I wore considerably. My body aroma was not near as strong as hers, or as attractive for that matter. Though I knew my confidence growing in my ability to protect myself outdoors also had something to do with it.

I had both the pistol and the fancy sword hanging from my belt. Cinnamon was weaponless except for her cutter, but I fully intended to keep her close. In a defensive situation I could always hand her the pistol, in hopes that she would be more valuable in a battle scenario than Coffee proved herself to be.

We completed the mist harvesting task without incident. It had become fairly routine. More birds gathered than usual as we went about that job. I took that as a good sign that there weren't any predators lurking nearby. They also appeared to be getting more used to human existence among them. Some even came within a few feet of us as they pecked at the ground in search of insects to eat.

Crows used to scare the shit out of me back on Earth when they got close. Some of these alien birds were even bigger than those. So far, though, they had not been overly aggressive. Compared to the wofurs and dragons, they were not much of a threat.

I was even starting to get used to the clicking noises that they made. Not an animal linguist by any means, I struggled to find variance in the length or tone of the clicks. Perhaps Teddy might know what the birds were saying. But would it even matter? What could they really have to talk about?

It brought to mind two cartoons from my time. In one, a boy developed a way to hear what his dog was saying. To no surprise, it wasn't much. *Throw the stick! Yay, he threw the stick. Here, I brought it back, throw it again.* In another, a different boy wore a contraption that allowed him to hear what all the animals were saying. When he overheard squirrels discussing current events and planning global manipulation, he nearly got himself killed.

I had no idea if Teddy had a special power of understanding animals, or if he had simply learned the language of some just like he did human galactic standard. I had not yet tested his claim that he could communicate with the other two caged beasts in the forward cargo hold. But I certainly planned to do so.

I spotted Gako sleeping on a low branch in his tree. Once we hauled all the gathered drinking water inside, I decided to go speak with him. Of course, I had no knowledge of dragon etiquette. Perhaps waking one was strictly taboo. Nonetheless, I figured that I'd give it a try. I invited Cinnamon to join me and was delightfully surprised that she accepted, though not without trepidation. She insisted on carrying the pistol.

The ground in this dragon populated world tended to be patchy. Most of the grass grew close to the bushes. Sometimes there was thick spongy moss in between them, and there was usually some around the trees. But the grass didn't grow much in the shade of the large red trees.

Circular sections of ground even out in the open held only firm dirt. It was like there used to be a trampoline park here. Not quite as shocking as crop circles, the formation of them did make me wonder how they were formed.

The roots of the huge red barked growth knuckled out of the ground making foot placement tricky. Patches of moss combined with divots full of bugs had us looking at the ground more than she should have. By the time we were within twenty feet of Gako's position he had already opened his eyes.

"What?" he asked. He was a dragon of few words.

"I'd like to talk," I told him as I ceased my approach. Cinnamon stood behind me, possibly waiting to be introduced. More likely she was afraid of the overgrown lizard that had the distinct scent of burnt antifreeze when he spoke. "If you don't mind."

Gako lifted his head off the branch with his long-scaled neck, blinking the sleep out of his eyes. I had caught him napping but he was able to notice our approach even without the ability to smell us. "Why?" he asked.

"I would like to ask your permission," I replied, speaking slowly. I wasn't sure if he could understand me when I spoke at normal speed, but human tendency was to mimic the people that you were talking to in order to improve communication. For all I knew it was offensive and insulting.

"Speak," he said then as he raised one clawed forward foot to scratch at the side of his neck just behind the head and ears.

"We need to move our ship before it falls off the cliff. I was wondering..."

"You," Gako started to say.

"What?"

"Picked bad spot," he finished his comment.

"Yes, they did," I laughed. "But not on purpose. They crashed. Now we..."

"They?" he asked. It took me a moment to figure out what he meant.

"Oh, yes, of course," I replied. I found myself speeding up my speech slightly in hopes of not being cut off. "I didn't arrive here on the ship with the rest of them. I came from someplace else." I debated on explaining that I was from another time and another planet, but that would just overly complicate things. Perhaps one day we would be sitting around playing dragon checkers, or whatever game we could enjoy together, and I would explain my whole life to him. Now was not the time.

I paused for a reply that never came. At least not until I opened my mouth to speak again.

"Oh," was all that he said.

"So, we would like to move the ship this way a bit," I told him. "Not real close, about halfway. But we need to take a lot of stuff out of the ship to make it lighter. The ground between the ship and your tree is reasonably flat and free of bushes, so it is only logical, to me at least, to stack the stuff close to the tree..."

"What?" Gako asked again.

"Oh, my stars," Cinnamon muttered from behind me.

God dammit! Was I going to have to repeat everything? I guessed that speaking slowly was a good idea after all. I should simplify things, too. He didn't need to know the back story or our reasons for our decisions.

"What do you want?" Gako asked when I didn't reply immediately. "From me?"

"Oh, I just want to put stuff on the ground over here," I gestured to the area just beyond the reach of the massive tree's branches. "After we move the ship this way, we pull it back from the tree a bit. I'm just trying to be a nice neighbor and tell you ahead of time. I didn't want any misunderstanding."

"I see," Gako responded.

"Oh, good," I said in relief. "I was worried that..."

"No," the dragon said then. "I need to see."

"Oh," Cinnamon said as she stepped up to my side. "Kash, he needs to be able to see his surroundings from his perch. He doesn't want us to block his view."

"Okay," I reacted by glancing back toward the ship. "We'll have to keep everything single stacked then, leaving plenty of visibility between the low branches and our cargo cubes."

"I not watch," Gako then told me.

"Oh, it is okay if you want to watch us moving the stuff," I answered him. "If we put anything where you don't like just let me know and we'll move it..."

"No," Gako said.

"Stars, Kash," Cinnamon the said as she placed her hand on my arm, gripping my wrist gently with her slender fingers. "I thought you were the dragon communicator, or whisperer as you called it. Gako is telling us that he won't watch over our cargo for us. We can't hold him responsible for it."

"Yes," Gako said, lowering his head like a human would slump their shoulders. Maybe he was getting frustrated with me.

"I'm Cinnamon, by the way," she introduced herself. Maybe I should have done so earlier.

Gako inhaled sharply before saying, "I know you by scent. You are Kash's female?"

"Ummm..."

"Yes," I answered for her. "She is my woman, under my protection."

Cinnamon didn't disagree. I wasn't sure if it was because of my phrasing or if she was agreeable to being considered my woman. I just wanted to make it clear to Gako that he should feel the same way toward her as he does me. A friend, to be protected.

"I hope better," Gako told us. We waited for more words to help us understand. "Than mine."

"You have a wife?" I asked in shock. I hadn't considered that possibility, even though the data suggested that the green dragons often traveled in pairs. Based on his comment maybe they were divorced or separated. Or whatever dragons did when they felt like they were not longer compatible.

"Female dragon," Gako corrected me, as if I meant that he had a human wife. "Very annoying."

Cinnamon made a noise like she was about to be defensive of all female kind. Or maybe she was stifling laughter like me. Either way, she didn't say anything.

"Will we ever meet her? Will she be friends with us, too?"

"Yes," Gako answered. "No."

Huh?

"You may meet her," the dragon explained. "She won't like you, Kash. But she might like your woman."

"I look forward to meeting her," Cinnamon said politely. The perfect diplomatic reply. I was seriously reconsidering my plans, once again. My favorite dirty girl could indeed be someone that I'd like to keep close to me, like a king keeps his queen. Especially if she could befriend a second dragon that already had loyalty to the first.

"Feed her," Gako said. "When she comes, give her big food."

"Oh, sure," Cinnamon replied. We might have to kill another wofur, or a small dragon to accomplish that.

"So, she doesn't eat you, Cinn-a-mon," Gako then told her. I didn't quite like the way that he licked his lips after what he said. Other than that, I thought the whole thing went pretty well.

The two of us made our way back toward the ship, pointing out the best places to put the cargo units and the mist harvesters as we went. We were nearly to the entrance when Cinnamon said, "I'm okay with it."

"With befriending Gako's wife?" I asked. "Thanks. She could be a huge asset to our survival here, just like Gako."

"Yes, that too," she answered. "But I was referring to being called your woman. I'm okay with it among the dragons, but not on the ship. Not just yet."

CHAPTER TWELVE:

"So, how did that go?" Strawberry asked from her position on the stairs. Without me knowing beforehand, she was prepared to come to our rescue should things have gone sour. The energy rifle sat beside her, butt on the floor, barrel to the ceiling leaning against the pale skin of her left knee.

Her ass was more than a little big for her petite frame. Her thighs had to compensate by tapering from narrow above the knees to quite thick at the hips. Even with her knees a good ten inches apart her thighs touched each other right at the bottom of her shorts.

Strawberry was small breasted, which perfectly matched her slim upper half. The closure to her top was left open much lower than normal, revealing some nicely freckles titties almost over to the nipple. She honestly looked like she had been posing for our entrance. I was fairly sure that was for my benefit and not that of Cinnamon.

I hesitated as I took in the scene, reaping a wide smile from her. She was certainly pleased with herself. "Better than I expected," I eventually stated.

"Good," she said as she leaned forward. I watched eagerly for at least one rosy red nipple to make an appearance, but neither did. "I think Honeysuckle has something to discuss with Cinnamon, but I'd like to hear from you more about this dragon conversation."

Strawberry gestured toward the maintenance area of the lower level. Cinnamon went without saying a word, but she gave me a backward glance that showed concern. Was she worried about my safety or another woman coming into to play? I was almost wanting her to start showing signs of jealousy. It would make her seem more like a devoted wife.

"Gako has no problem with us placing cargo over by his tree as long as it doesn't block his view," I informed her.

"That's impressive," she said as she stood and edged uncomfortably close to me for a professional conversation. Then gesturing upstairs, she added, "We can discuss it more privately..."

"No," I cut her off. I didn't mean to be rude, but I wasn't interested in getting played either. I needed to think with my head and not my willy for a while. "I have some things to take care of down here."

"Okay," she replied, but did not move an inch to step out of my way. "I just want to make sure that you know that I have your back."

"I appreciate that," I answered, though I might not have come across as convincing as I intended. I was too busy trying to think why she would be saying these things.

"Maybe one day I can have your front as well."

"My front?"

She smiled again as she rubbed her dainty knuckles against the front of my shorts. "I'm a very unselfish lover," she told me softly. "I just want more than love in return."

I debated on asking her what the hell that meant. To get into her vagina did I need to sell my soul to the devil? Was she going to make me kill someone? Or was she seeking some kind of title, like best pussy onboard?

"Okay," I finally said as I took a cautious step back from her. She stared into my eyes as I did. I saw no lust there. She appeared to be calm, cool and collected. She was trying to make a play alright, but not necessarily for my loving. I nearly ran off without fully understanding the situation. This was my chance to build an alliance. She had indicated that she was interested in doing so ever since I saved her bubble butt from going over the edge of the cliff.

"I'm interested in working with you more," I chose my words carefully. "I'm sorry that I'm a little put off by your forward manner, but I'm up for discussing a mutually beneficial relationship soon. Just not this moment, here on the steps."

Strawberry nodded and reeled in her wide smile. "I apologize, Kash. I was under the impression that you were even hornier that our previous two men. But I can see now that there is a time and place for everything with you. That's as impressive as your ability to control your dragon. Let's talk again soon then."

"Yes," I nodded, glad that I had recovered and gained something from the brief conversation. "Soon. Maybe even later today, if it works out."

"I look forward to it," she replied as she turned and went up the steps. That's when I noticed the rifle resting against the railing. "Please put the gun away for me. I don't think we'll be needing it when we meet again."

Damn, I sure hope not.

I stored the rifle where it belonged and turned to find both Cinny and Honey staring at me. They appeared to be more concerned for my welfare than my complicated love life, so I assured them that everything was okay before proceeding into the forward hold.

I went straight to the keypad on Teddy's cage and released the bars. He joined me for a seat against the food crate without hesitation this time. Though still grumpy by nature he appeared to be in much better spirits since he agreed to this new relationship between us.

"What can I do for you, Kash?"

"I'm curious about this ability of yours to speak to the other animals. Is that some kind of special skill? Do all of your kind have it?"

"It is not a superpower, if that is what you are asking. My people are a little more intuitive than yours apparently. I did complete brain function courses with honors, so I am a bit better than average at least."

"Awesome," I told him. I assumed that brain function courses were like college on Earth. And maybe spell classes for witches and mind reading classes for the telepathic. "I'm curious what the Tigritari and the Savrad have to say. Have you had long conversations with them?"

"Oh, no," Teddy responded with a wave of his hand that mimicked human gesture. "Nothing like that. Neither of these beasts are near our level of intelligence."

"The Tigritari," he continued. "Their kind live on several planets, and my home world is one of them. I believe that they were imported for breeding and selling the offspring on these space stations that I've heard about. They are quite expensive. They can't communicate much, but I'm able to understand them fairly well. Giving them instructions in their language is tricky, but it can be done. They respond better when their words are combined with hand gestures that they can learn. That is how their owners learn to control them as pets."

"I see," I replied. "Hey, before we go any farther, does your kind typically wear clothes?"

"Yes!" Teddy answered excitedly. It was almost an outburst compared to his regular demeanor. "I am not fond of being kept naked, especially for the viewing of your females."

"Well," I shrugged, "It's not like they are interested in... Uh, do you have the same...?"

"Yes, Kash. I have a penis. I have been informed by the one that you call Coffee that mine is infinitesimally small compared to yours, though."

"Well, it would have to be, really. Or it would be dragging the floor." His short legs honestly weren't much longer than my full-on erection.

"She indicated that as well," he said almost angrily. "I don't know anything about average human penis size, but she seemed to be very impressed with yours."

"That's good news," I laughed as I thought back to my episode of sexual intercourse with the dark-skinned beauty. The penetration that I supplied did appear to be more than sufficient to get the job done.

"If we may get back to the subject of clothes," Teddy said with a unique expression that indicated he knew what I was thinking about. "I would be immensely appreciative if you would supply some. Mine were stripped of me shortly after my capture, and I highly doubt that any were supplied for my transport. Is this vessel equipped with a garment maker?"

"A garment maker?" I laughed. "Dude, there are only like six women on this ship. They may have a way of making clothes, but I kind of doubt it. They are all wearing the same uniforms that their previous captain required."

"I did notice the lack in fashion variety."

"But I'm sure that we can figure something out," I told him. "It might not fit well, though. In fact, instead of pants you could essentially have to wear something that looks like a diaper."

"Fuck you, Kash," Teddy murmured.

"Excuse me?" I coughed and laughed at the same time. I couldn't really take offense. The diaper comment had to come across as an insult. I should have said loincloth instead.

"Thank you, Kash," Teddy said more clearly. "I would appreciate any clothes that you could manage."

"No problem, Teddy," I told him. Though it was a brief conversation I could feel our bond growing already, and his dependence on me. "How about the Savrad? Have you communicated with it?'

"Minimally," Teddy responded, almost with a slight British accent. I wasn't sure what the hell that was about. Maybe he learned the word that way. "I don't recommend ever releasing it."

"Oh, really? That bad, huh?"

"That beast is very angry," Teddy told me. "I'm not familiar with that species, so they could all be that way as far as I know. Judging by its confidence I would say that the heavy pointed tail is quite dangerous. Given the opportunity, it would kill everyone onboard before going off to fight one of these dragons that you claim exist outside the ship."

"Claim?"

"I am not suggesting that you are lying," Teddy raised his hands in an apologetic, take no offense nature. "I am just saying that I have not seen these creatures for myself, or any evidence of their existence. I am trusting solely on your word, which I am obliged to believe."

"Damn, Teddy," I said. He made me feel like a country hick by the way he talked. "You make things harder than they need to be sometimes."

"I shall work on that," he responded humbly. His demeanor was softening with each visit. I was sure that he had some pent-up anger himself. Maybe some relative freedom would relieve that.

"Would you prefer to be allowed to roam this room?" I asked as I stood. Our little visit was over. I needed to get back to work. I didn't have the luxury of extended breaks. Nobody ever climbed through the ranks by sitting in a cargo hold talking extensively to an alien captive. At least, I didn't think so.

"It doesn't matter much," Teddy replied as he also rose up onto his feet. It made extraordinarily little difference in his height from the seated position. "Other than access to the food container, there is no real benefit. I can remain in my cage while you are away if that works better for you."

"Thanks," I told him genuinely. "I think it does." I opened the cargo hold door and began to walk through it when I had a thought. Teddy was being very appreciative and useful. I needed to reward him in some way. It would be good for our relationship going forward.

"I don't like to make promises that I can't keep," I told the small alien koala teddy bear. "But if all goes well, you'll be walking through this door tomorrow. Not forever. Just for a stroll, I think. How does that sound?"

Teddy nodded forward like some kind of Asian dignitary from my time. Was that the custom of his people, or did he pick that up off of a human also? His pause after righting himself seemed a bit emotional. Finally, he answered.

"I would like that very much, Kash."

CHAPTER THIRTEEN:

It was a grueling long day of work with tons of studying on top of it. I had that combined tired thing going on. Not just physically tired, or mentally drained, but both. Still, I was committed to do all that I could as fast as I could. I needed to be prepared for whatever opportunities lie ahead.

On a beached boat with six exotic beautiful women, you would think that I'd be super chatty at the dinner table. And normally I was. Tonight, though, I had chosen to bring my tablet to the table in the galley. I wasn't the first one to do it, but on this occasion, I was the only one.

I had seen Cinnamon, Honeysuckle and Strawberry regularly scrolling through reports as they ate. I, however, studied each screen completely before proceeding to the next. Sometimes, I forgot to eat. Once I held my fork in the air for two full minutes with a cube of meat as I studied the screen. It wasn't until the girls started snickering that I realized what I was doing.

"You are working too hard," Strawberry told me with a sexy secretary vibe. Only Sage and Vanilla were missing from the small gathering for the late evening meal. Those two tended to eat earlier and retire to their quarters before the rest of us even got ourselves cleaned up for the evening.

"He's just trying to do more than his share," Cinnamon came to my defense. "He feels like he has some catching up to do."

"Maybe in some ways he does," Strawberry replied honestly. "But for the most part, his performance has been exemplary."

Exemplary? Did Strawberry just pay me a huge compliment in front of the others?

"You would think as the only male onboard," Honeysuckle said as she was finishing off her dessert. Everyone had already finished their main course except for me. "He'd be sitting back and watching us women do all the work. Just like Captain King used to do."

"Well," Strawberry replied as she crossed her slender but shapely arms across her chest. "He isn't the captain." There was a pause where I was worried that one of my friends would say something out of line, like *he ain't the captain yet*. But no one did. "But as the only male you would expect a lot more arrogance for sure. I have to give him a great degree of respect for that."

"That is definitely true," Cinnamon added. The sound of her higher pitch voice singing my praise pulled me away from my train of thought. My attempt to study was getting sabotaged.

"He's a rare and very special man," Coffee then said as she slipped her arm around my waist. She had already finished her meal, disposed of her dish and sat back down beside me with no apparent purpose other than to continue socializing. I felt her tiny breasts push against my arm the same time that her lips contacted my shoulder.

That was undeniably my cue.

I powered off the tablet and shoved my last bite of veggie roll into my mouth. Rotating my body, I raised my right arm high in the air to place it around Coffee's tiny frame. Then I glanced around to see the response from the others. Strawberry was grinning. Honeysuckle smiled shyly then turned to leave. Cinnamon was plainly ignoring us. Perhaps there was a bit of jealousy there after all.

"I like how you fit right in around here," Coffee said in a low voice. It was clear that she intended the rest of the conversation to be just between us. "Not like one of the girls, of course. One of the crew. You don't act like the galaxy owes you something."

"I don't believe that it does," I responded as I gave her my full attention. The other two then stood up from the table and said their good nights. It was unlikely that I would see either of them again before bedtime. My acceptance of Coffee's attention limited my prospects for the night. With her looking like my best chance to get lucky, I was decidedly fine with that.

"Honestly," I told her as I watched the pulsing of intricate lines across her neck and chest. "I feel very privileged to be here. Things could have gone so much worse for me."

Coffee smiled at me like she wasn't paying attention. Then after the words sunk in, she said, "Oh yeah, coming through a portal to a strange alien world. I'm surprised that they didn't give you more equipment to help keep you alive. Did you expect this to be a suicide mission?"

"Kind of," I answered as I tried to remember what all I had revealed so far. Most of my lies were simply substituting being an astronaut for being a prisoner. Of course, that also meant that I had a choice of whether to go through the portal or not. Technically I did.

"We knew that if I landed on another habitable planet that I would die of old age before a rescue attempt could be made. If instead I was transported to a different location on Earth, the beacon that I set up could help them find me quickly as long as I didn't end up deep in a cave somewhere. The real issue is the time lapse, though. If my signal could even break through the atmosphere of this planet it will be hundreds of years before the people of Earth would know of my survival."

Coffee pulled back and looked me in the eye. "Do you think that your beacon signal is strong enough to alert other ships to our location?"

"I highly doubt it," I replied. "Certainly, technology has advanced exponentially since my beacon was made."

"Yes, but our signal stopped sending after our crash," Coffee explained as she glanced at both doorways to the galley. Was this another secret being revealed? "The captain was working with Honeysuckle to repair the problem. It was almost fixed when he died. Since then, Sage won't let us focus on getting the system working again."

"I thought that the signal couldn't penetrate the alien atmosphere here," I told her.

"We don't know that for sure," Coffee whispered. "Scanning a surface for details requires more clarity than a simple outgoing message."

I added this new information to my mental mystery notebook. Had Sage sabotaged the ship, then prevented an outgoing message that could get them rescued? Did she also kill, or get killed, the captain and the pilot? What was her goal in doing all of this? It couldn't be worth the risk of being stranded on this dangerous planet with the ship teetering on the edge of a cliff just to move up in the ranks. Could it?

The truth was that I didn't really know these people. They themselves admitted that the lifestyle and mentality of most humans had changed significantly over the last few decades. Maybe everyone was cutthroat these days.

That was okay with me, given my background. I hung around with shady types since my teens, then went to prison. I was more prepared for a dog-eat-dog society than most time travelers would be. But it was just so disappointing.

After stumbling upon six attractive women in a vulnerable situation with no men around, I had allowed myself to have high hopes. One at a time, acquire all six of them as lovers. Then rise up to become their captain. Get the ship fixed and do some exploring. Flaunt my good luck a bit, maybe find even more sexy girls to join the crew. We had eight crew quarters and just seven of us. Double bunking was a real possibility, especially if we worked in shifts. I personally would be agreeable to triple bunking with the right pair of women.

"Kash, are you okay?" Coffee asked me, sounding sincerely worried about my blank stare.

"Yes, I'm just trying to think about what all this means."

"What it means is that we can boost your beacon to send a signal for help," she explained, rolling down a completely different line of thought than me. "Sage won't be able to notice it since it won't show up on a ship's systems report. All communications we receive go through me, so I can hide it from her easily."

That did sound feasible. The only problem was that I wasn't quite ready to be rescued. Of course, sending the signal didn't guarantee that someone would hear it and coming looking for us. However, helping Coffee with this project would surely bring us closer together. It could also help me break my followers even further away from Sage's control.

If I could manage to get three or four of the six women to obey me, I could certainly gain control of the situation. Within reason, of course.

I had no plans to dominate them like a tyrant. Just have them follow my lead. Add a dragon as my friend, and an intuitive little alien creature that speaks English. Or galactic standard. My plan was coming together. I had to seize this opportunity.

"I have two beacons," I told her. "I set one up before I met Cinnamon. The other one was still in my bag when I arrived here. It went missing, though, while I was being held like a prisoner."

"I bet Cinnamon knows where it is," Coffee said excitedly. "She probably was told to secure it in a locker on the lower level. Let's go ask her!"

"No, no," I replied, gesturing for her to lower her voice. We didn't want anyone to overhear this plan of ours. "We'll do it in the morning at a time that won't draw anyone's attention."

Coffee looked a little disappointed with my statement. I wasn't expecting that. My plan was to keep her clinging to me for help and guidance in both rescue and survival matters.

"So," she said tentatively, "Are we done talking for tonight?"

"No!" I replied, louder than I should have. "I mean, not if you want to continue talking. I would love to spend more time with you. Have you ever been in the captain's quarters?"

"No," Coffee answered slyly. "Not really. Would you like to take this discussion to a more private location?"

I returned her ornery grin and nodded. *Yes, very much so*, I thought. Private time with Coffee could present a two-fold gain. A closer follower, and a dedicated lover. Plus, I just plainly wanted some good sex. Hanging around these gorgeous women after a few months in prison was almost torture when I couldn't get some release. I've done a lifetime's worth of jerking off ever since I was arrested.

The last time that the two of us entered a bedroom with sex on our mind Coffee had gotten right to business by pulling down her shorts to reveal her ass and pussy. Would she be that eager again?

I gestured for her to step inside first. Motioning for the door to close behind me I slid up against her back. She had been glancing around the room, but there wasn't much to see. I stowed everything from the previous occupant in the lockers and I had very few personal belongings myself.

Coffee leaned back into me gently. It was an invitation. Looking over her brown shoulder I watched as my hands tugged on her top to release the closure holding the two sides together. Unlike Velcro or magnets, the bond released smoothly with the right amount of pressure applied to specific points.

Coffee laid her head back on to my shoulder and chuckled as I fondled her tiny breasts in the most controlled manner that I could manage. When she kissed me on the cheek, I turned to place my lips on hers. The strong taste of chocolate mint filled my mouth as I plunged my tongue between her teeth.

I could feel Coffee pulling her pants down, then raising each leg to send them to the floor. When she pulled on one wrist, I assumed that she was ready for me to give her pussy some attention. I was delighted to oblige.

My erection was growing firm against her ass, but my shorts were still in the way. I didn't want to stop touching her to release my monster, so I was hoping that she would do it. However, she was way too caught up in her own pleasure.

I continued to kiss her mouth, cheek and shoulder as I rubbed her clit and fingered her tight hole up to the second knuckle on just one finger. Her breath was getting heavy already.

"I want to eat it again," I whispered in her ear. Hopefully, she knew what that meant and wasn't expecting me to ingest a part of her body.

Coffee giggled excitement at my comment then replied, "And I want to suck your cock off this time." I was fairly sure that she didn't mean to literally remove it from my body. It was weird which expressions stood the test of time and which faded into the past. Caution was needed occasionally, especially where my manhood was concerned.

I pulled back so I could remove my clothes and boots. She took the opportunity to pull off her footwear as well, then bend over to show me her delicious pussy again. It was already glistening in the dim light of my cabin. Apparently, she wanted to go first again. But I had a better idea.

I reached between her slender thighs with both arms to grab the front of her hips. Raising back to a standing position I flipped her upside down, her sexy legs spreading as they flew into the air. She squealed, but quickly understood what I was doing. My strong arms clamped around her narrow waist to hold her in a vertical sixty-nine position.

The maneuver placed her moist pink vagina hole right on the dinner table for me. I felt my cock rub against the tough strands of her blonde hair first. Then she grabbed it with one hand as she steadied herself with the other on my knee. I was lapping away at her pussy for a while before she managed to get her mouth around the head of my penis.

I licked and sucked vigorously as she struggled to keep up. Between gasping she would suck strongly on my tip at times while stroking the shaft. Other times she would plunge her mouth down to engulf at least half of my meat. I knew that most women gave their best head while they were receiving oral attention themselves. Others, like Coffee, became a bit more erratic due to a loss of focus.

It shocked me at how quickly her thighs clamped to the sides of my head. The way her body was convulsing I knew that she was having a full-on orgasm, but I couldn't hear her with my ears trapped. She might have been screaming for me to stop. I just couldn't bring myself to pull my mouth away until I was sure. Her legs flailing around, then a couple kicks to my skull finally got the message across.

I pulled my mouth back from her drenched crevice. She had cum so much that it was running down her ass crack onto her back. She was going to get her secretion in her own hair if I continued to hold her upside down.

"Aaaghh!" she screamed as her legs vibrated out of control. I was planning to put her down gently onto the bed when I felt her mouth and both hands go to work on my boner again. I couldn't see what she was doing, but it felt amazing.

My tip hit something solid several times. Her gagging afterwards confirmed that she was going deep enough on me that it was striking the back of her throat. Her desire to do so much to get me off was extremely arousing.

"Oh, fuck," I said. "Coffee, I'm going... I'm going to..."

Her mouth stopped abruptly and became a human vacuum cleaner. It was as if she was trying to suck the head right off. If I wasn't at the beginning of a powerful orgasm I would have been concerned. Both of her tiny hands worked feverishly to stroke the lower shaft. I couldn't hold off any longer.

Pain shot through my body along with intense pleasure. My climax was so over the top that it hurt, but in a good way. She continued as I stood there shuddering. If it weren't for my arm muscles clenched like a vice, I would have dropped her. It wasn't until she believed that she had extracted every drop of my semen that she released her grip on my exhausted yogurt slinger.

I expected her to scream when she pushed against my thighs for me to release her waist. Then I remembered that her mouth was still full of my most treasured gift. It wasn't until she was seated upright that she managed to swallow it all.

I felt like collapsing on the bed beside her. Her intense upside-down blowjob drained me in more ways than one. I was extremely appreciative, and I planned to tell her so, after I laid down.

She grabbed my hips, though, preventing me from diving onto the bed. With psychotic laughter she began stroking my cock again. It was still reasonably hard but trending the other way until she started tugging on it.

"Get hard again," Coffee demanded from my loins. "I need it, Kash. I have to have it inside me."

I watched in amazement as my penis firmed up in her hand. Her tongue wickedly lapping away at my balls helped considerably. I didn't understand why, though. My genitals should be as tired and in need of rest as I was.

Once Coffee was satisfied with the condition of my revived boner she quickly flipped around and pointed her ass at it. She guided the tip to the hottest, wettest pussy that I had ever felt, then shoved her body backwards forcibly.

"Fuck!" she screamed. She probably should have taken it slower.

My mind was trying to adjust. My cock was getting fucked by possibly the most dazzling woman that I had ever been with in my life. Despite my firmness, I was struggling to get into it at first.

As she continued to slam her firm ass cheeks against my pelvis the appropriate chemicals started flowing again. I grabbed her narrow waist and did my best to contribute. She didn't really need my help. She began screaming again as I felt a rush of fluid surround my shaft and splash onto my balls. She was cumming again already.

Her motion slowed, then, but I took over the power thrusting. I soon climaxed again myself, though not as dramatically as the first time. I was sure that my testicles did not have adequate time to brew up another large batch of creamy white goodness. Releasing inside of her I couldn't know for sure. However, her fluids were enough to make a big enough mess to obliterate mine.

We ignored the slick floor and wet side of the bed as we tumbled into each other's arms on the mattress. A few tender kisses with our eyes closed, then we both fell asleep. I was exhausted but also very gratified. An overwhelming happiness swept across me as I drifted off with Coffee in my arms.

I wanted to sing one of my perverted songs in my head, but everything was coming across as a lullaby instead. I dozed off before I could manage to sing a single verse.

CHAPTER FOURTEEN:

Teddy marched through the ship as dignified as he could manage. His limited height was a challenge, as was the poorly stitched new trousers that drug the floor despite being cuffed up. We had misjudged where his hips would hold the waistband of the pants. The vest, however, was giving him a totally cool alien space pirate vibe. Both pieces of clothing had been made from a shiny black material in one of the cargo cubes.

He glanced at the two cargo holds as he quickly passed through, needing to take at least five steps to match every one of mine. I pointed out Honeysuckle's repair section. The green skinned playful young woman smiled at him as she waved, taking a brief break from what she was doing to lend some encouragement. I knew that she would approve of letting Teddy go for a walk through the ship.

I pointed out the doorway to the engine room and supply lockers off to the side. Per my conversation with Coffee and Cinnamon I knew that the beacon that had been taken from my backpack was locked in the third unit from the left. I would retrieve it soon under the guise of looking for something else. Anytime a locked door, cabinet or tablet application was unlocked, the computer would create an alert. It was unknown if Sage was tracking something as minor as locker openings.

Each step to the upper level was about eight inches high, just like the standard I was used to back on Earth. I expected my new friend to struggle with climbing them. He was after all just twenty-five inches tall. His arms, though, from shoulder to fingertip were nearly twenty inches long. Strong muscles for his size enabled him to launch himself up the staircase in quick fashion.

His orange fuzzy appearance in poorly fitting black clothing made him look like a puppet from television in the twentieth century. Anyone from my time upon first encounter would likely look for the strings of the puppet master, or the human hand up his ass.

Teddy stood patiently at the top until both Coffee and I had joined him. His method had him ascend surprisingly fast. I had a brief vision of him grabbing a knife somewhere and running through the hallways like an evil doll from a horror movie. But Teddy was smart. He knew to respect his limited freedom if wanted to ever be let out again.

Neither Sage nor Vanilla had been informed of my mischievous act. I did let Strawberry know to see what she would do with the information. She could have insisted against us letting Teddy upstairs at all. Or she might have ran to tell Sage on me. Instead, to my delight, she offered to keep her leader busy for ten minutes to give us ample time for a quick walk through.

The doctor typically spent long shifts in her lab during the day unless she was needed elsewhere. We figured it was best to just leave her out of the loop completely.

Cinnamon was concerned that this frivolous act would set Sage off in a way that could cause issues with our future plans. I, however, figured this was one of those no harm, no foul situations. I trusted Teddy to be well behaved. There was nothing to lose by letting him see the interior of the ship that just might end up being his coffin if it went over the cliff.

We hustled by the door to the medical bay without drawing any attention, then led Teddy into the galley. He took a long look at the food processors with photos of the type of edibles available above it. It was the first time that I realized that he might be unsatisfied with his diet. The crew had essentially been feeding him a small variety of dog biscuits for weeks.

When he slowly turned to me, I half expected a twitching evil eye and steam coming out of his ears. To his credit, Teddy stayed calm and cool as he spoke to me.

"I would love the opportunity to earn a meager portion of your rations," he said without any malice. I was quickly getting used to his naturally unhappy tone. He didn't come across any grumpier than usual.

"We'll have to work that out with Strawberry," I told him. I was fairly sure that she would be okay with it, but what could Teddy do for us to earn some good food? "We might have to eventually build you a high-chair to join us for dinner," I said jokingly.

The short alien studied the seating situation and nodded as he mumbled something under his breath. He probably was not appreciative of my comment, but smart enough not to show it.

"What did he say?" Coffee asked me.

"I said," Teddy addressed her for the first time since coming on board. He had previously refused to speak to our females and only revealed that he could even speak our language when I asked him a question. "I said that I doubt that I'll be joining you for dinner soon. I'm sure that most of your crew still considers me a lowly pet or a dumb animal."

I hurried our threesome out of the galley and around the hallway. Strawberry might be exiting Sage's room any minute. Though I wasn't severely worried about repercussions, I just as soon avoid conflict when possible.

I had told Teddy that he would need to show respect for the other women on this ship. His reply to Coffee even though she had asked me the question suggests that he was willing to comply with that requirement.

"For your information," Coffee whispered from behind Teddy. "Some of us don't see you as an animal anymore since you started talking. The others don't even know that you are intelligent. If you had spoken to us before..."

"Oh, my stars!" Vanilla screamed out as she rounded the corner by the stairwell. The landing there was a shortcut from her medical facility to the toilets. She just had to pick that exact moment to have a pee.

The doctor jumped back a step at the sight of Teddy strolling through the ship like an ape-armed toddler. The small alien simply stopped and waited to see how I would handle the situation. In that moment, though, he looked Vanilla's body up and down before saying, "Hello, doctor."

I motioned for Coffee to lead Teddy back downstairs urgently in case Vanilla's shock had alerted the others. Cabin doors were very dense, but not completely soundproof. The super sexy medic was quite loud with her scream.

"Are the toilets in there?" Teddy asked as Coffee was waving him to go faster. "I need to pee. Perhaps the good doctor could show me how to..."

Vanilla screamed sharply again as the fuzzy orange guy passed by just inches from her. She had backed up against the wall, but hallways on spaceships were understandably narrow. Seeing Teddy wave to her as he was led away was nearly comical. Was he attracted to a human female?

"You are too small for our toilets," Coffee explained in a loud whisper as she pointed down the stairs. I had informed her not to touch the guy under any circumstances. Being pushed by a woman would likely be beyond what his ego could bare.

"Is everything okay out here?" Strawberry said shortly after the door to Sage's cabin slid open. She stepped out into the hallway to barely catch a glimpse of Teddy's backside as he began descending to the lower level.

"Yes, we're fine," I replied as I slid up against Vanilla to pull her away from the wall. I needed her to recover from her shock as quickly as possible. This was a defining moment in our relationship. Would she announce that an alien had intentionally been let loose onboard? Or would she cover for me?

Sage's head popped out of the doorway to her quarters. "Vanilla? Are you okay?"

"Yes," Vanilla answered as she composed herself. "Sorry about that. I had my head down as I rounded the corner here and nearly bumped into Kash."

The doctor gave me a look that suggested that I now owe her one. Given my sexual release in her presence twice now, I figured that I owed her more. The question was how could I repay her? Keeping the secret that she had touched me while I was unconscious may have been enough before. I would have to think about that later.

"What are you doing up here, Kash?" Sage asked like I was the instigator of the problem.

I made a gesture like I was holding my penis, and answered, "I had to pee."

Sage shook her head at my behavior and retreated into her room. Strawberry's smile suggested that I owed her as well. My debts were racking up. I needed to start paying them if I was going to completely win them over.

Then I remembered that I had saved Strawberry's ass from going over the cliff as Sage simply watched. She should still be indebted to me. Her confidence would not allow her to show that, even if she did feel that way. A conversation was definitely needed soon with the fiery redhead to get us more firmly connected.

When I returned to the cargo hold Teddy was already sitting in his cage. Coffee hadn't locked him in or shut the door to the forward hold. She was waiting outside for my signal in case our leader had followed me down the stairs.

"It's okay," I told Coffee. "Vanilla didn't let the cat out of the bag."

My dark-skinned lover gave me the queerest expression and she mouthed the words that I had just said. I should have known that phrase had faded away long ago.

"I hope that I did not cause a massive disturbance among your crew," Teddy said to me. "I appreciate the walk. It felt really good to get about the ship."

"You are welcome," I replied. "We'll try a longer visit next time."

"Perhaps," Teddy said with a tone that I had not heard from him before. "Perhaps I could be examined by the doctor. It might make the other females more comfortable with my presence."

That was a valid point. I had to be examined when I came on board. You would think that an alien being allowed contact with the crew should be an even bigger risk. But somehow the way that he spoke made his request sound naughty.

"Oh, my stars," Coffee uttered. "Teddy, don't tell me that you have a boner for Vanilla, too!"

Teddy briefly looked down at his crotch area before placing both hands in front of it. He did not need to reply. My suspicions had been correct. I pictured the little orange fucker jerking off into a bedpan as he lusted after Vanilla's breasts, lips, and possibly her unusual ears. Then I quickly shook my head to get the vision out of my mind.

"Kash?" I heard Cinnamon's higher pitched voice calling to me from the main cargo hold. "When you are done in there, I have something for you."

Both Coffee and Teddy gave me a look that indicated my best friend was referring to something sexual. I tried to laugh it off, but my eagerness betrayed me. I rushed out to find my Cinny standing there smiling with one hand on her hip. In her other hand was an object.

The beacon from my backpack.

CHAPTER FIFTEEN:

Over the next few days, we made a lot of progress. Everyone but Sage got involved with the repair work. Some of it was simple tasks like patching holes. The training course for applying the sealing compound was just five minutes and mostly covered safety precautions. Other educational modules took hours to even skim over for the important parts.

I worked with Strawberry to coordinate a schedule that had us splitting our time between several projects with one goal in mind. By ready to move the ship farther from the cliff as quickly as possible.

Honeysuckle still handled most of the detailed work. But she did give Vanilla three futuristic circuit boards to repair. The doctor's steady hand was able to complete the assignment with minimal explanation on how to reconnect the tiny broken pathways.

Our mechanic did manage to find time to upgrade my outdated beacon with components to provide a stronger signal. Coffee got involved to code the proper distress signals in hopes that we could lure a good Samaritan to our rescue. I was informed that there was an equal chance that a crew with malicious intent could intercept our transmission. We would have to be prepared for that scenario as well.

Gako supplied protection as Cinnamon and I walked a distance to reach a high point to securely mount the beacon where it was less likely to get destroyed by the local wildlife. On the way back my dragon friend confessed that he was missing his female companion. He had not seen her in weeks and was worried about her safety. It seemed that seeing Cinnamon and I together, occasionally hand in hand, was stirring up emotions. By the time we returned to the ship Gako announced that he would go looking for her.

One afternoon after each essential person completed a repair assignment, we focused on moving the cargo cubes outside and placing them all together about a hundred feet away, near the big red tree. Most of the work was completed by the loader under Cinnamon's control. She was quite good at both manual and programmed manipulation of the heavy unit. Things like moving the mist harvesters, though, were too challenging for its simple configuration.

The loader came with several attachments that could be swapped as needed where a human's hands would be. I had only seen it used with the standard L-shaped lifters that were perfect for moving cargo units around. Cinnamon confessed that she rarely used anything else, though she had been trained on how to use them all.

There was a storage compartment in the back of the loader where these attachments could be stored for easy access. It couldn't hold them all, but three or four might fit depending on the individual pieces.

Loader attachments included drills, saws, hooks, pushers, punchers and grippers that were almost like hands. There was also a shovel that could be used to scrape the top layer of ground away and provide a flat surface for the base.

For the purpose of moving cargo Cinnamon left the L-lifters attached. The broad square base of the unit was equipped with a rugged ball foot on each corner. What I had not previously realized was that each foot was mounted to a retractable leg. The massive robotic unit could easily traverse the rough terrain outside the ship and even climb steps if needed.

The ship had a dozen collapsible boxes about four-foot square and two feet high. They were made of an incredibly strong but thin type of plastic that was reportedly awfully expensive. All of them were folded up and stored in a section by the lockers no bigger than a broom closet. We used them to hold anything we wanted taken outside that wasn't already stored in cargo units.

Our computer-generated risk of the ship slipping over the edge of the cliff reduced to near nothing as we continued to move heavy objects out of it. Coffee and Cinnamon suggested that we just leave the ship where it was and start building our outdoor base. But I had seen firsthand how precarious our position was with the shattered debris beneath us. I agreed with Sage when she dismissed that notion and announced that our plan of using the thrusters would continue.

I let Teddy out twice a day to roam the ship. He mostly stayed in the lower level to avoid problems. Strawberry informed me that Sage had indeed taken notice and was about to put a stop to it. My freckled red-haired new friend claimed that she discouraged her leader from taking any action. Having the funny, in a grumpy way, alien moving among them had been a bit of a morale boost. Something away from the normal routine of survival here on dragon world.

We never let Teddy outside, though. Something told me that the possibility for him to run off was still there, though very slim. Losing a valuable piece of their goods for sale like that would be a huge blow to my standing with crew. I knew that Sage still planned to sell Teddy to the highest bidder on the next station, should we ever manage to get off this planet. In reality, that was still probably a better prospect than running for freedom here. Even if he could survive on this world with all its predators, it would not be an enjoyable life. He'd be completely alone, unless he managed to befriend a dragon like I had.

It was an extremely exciting day when enough repairs had been completed to fire up the engines. All crew except Honeysuckle and Vanilla positioned themselves in the control room as we monitored systems. Our mechanic was stationed in the engine room in case something went terribly wrong and needed a manual override.

Strawberry told me to sit beside her as she fed the same screens of information to my station that she was viewing. I couldn't tell if Sage approved or was just tolerating it. I knew when the time came to move the ship laterally to a safer location, I would be needed in the pilot's chair. Even though I was just learning the controls, there was no one more qualified than me for the job left alive.

We watched as most of the system checks turned green on the screen. Only two returned a failure message in red. I was disappointed, but Strawberry seemed happy that there weren't more. That was the first notion that I received that she did not have full confidence in our mechanic. Perhaps that was the reason for the barrier between those two.

It wasn't until the engines were powered down that we heard and felt a second rumble.

"What is that?" Coffee asked as the rest of us carefully stood still. We knew what it was. The ship was shifting again.

"Twenty-three percent chance of losing the ship off the cliff," Cinnamon announced with a controlled panic in her voice. "That's the highest that it has been in a while."

We all acknowledged her concern. We were right there with her. Only the rumbling hadn't stopped yet.

"Your little fur ball down below is probably scared shitless," Sage said. She was trying to get a rise out of me, but it was honestly a fair statement. Anyone that didn't have a data screen in front of them had no idea how we were faring.

Eventually, the shifting of our space boat ceased, and everyone let out a heavy breath. Cinnamon then announced that the threat actually went down in probability. I wasn't sure how that worked, but the screen said only a seventeen percent chance of falling into the canyon.

"Two system failures," Strawberry told the group. "All things considered, not bad. I'd call it a success."

Sage rolled her eyes at her second in command. Apparently, she was not in the mood for optimism.

"Honeysuckle!" Sage called for the mechanic through the ship's intercom. "How is it looking down there? We show two failures. I need an update quickly."

"Yes," Honey's voice came through the speakers embedded in the corners of the ceiling. The sound quality was amazing, though, and made it appear as though the mechanic was standing in the room with us. "Minor issues, I believe. We should be able to try again in an hour or two. Are we stable?"

"Stable enough," Sage replied. "Do what you have to do. We'll try again after lunch." With that Sage released the restraint on her seat, which I previously did not know existed, and walked calmly from the room.

"Good job everybody!" Strawberry's enthusiasm struck me as a bit over the top. When no one answered, she said as she too rose from her seat, "Come on people! The engines work and we didn't die. That's a cause for a celebration!"

"Yeah," I said weakly in comparison to her. But we were going to be trying again in a couple hours. It wasn't like we should break out the nanite whiskey.

I jumped slightly when Strawberry placed her arms around my shoulders. Her lips against my cheek were an even bigger shock. But nothing compared to when she twisted my left nipple through my t-shirt.

"Kash, your plans worked!" Strawberry explained the reason for the attention that she was giving me. Maybe where she was from, a place called Crimson Loop Station Centauri, titty twisting was a common form of celebration. I was tempted to reach around quickly and twist hers. You know, when in Rome, twist nipples like the Romans do.

"Okay, you poopers," Strawberry said, obviously disappointed with our reactions. I was surprised that *pooper* of all terms was still around. Though this was the first time that I heard it uttered. "I'm going to eat lunch, rub one out, then I'll see all your beautiful faces back in here after that."

She darted from the room quickly as we all looked at each other. "Did she say that she is going to rub one out?" Cinnamon asked. "What does that mean?"

Coffee laughed, then demonstrated by rubbed her pussy through her shorts with one hand and her breast with the other. If that wasn't comical enough, she licked her lips wildly and rolled her eyes like she was having a demonic orgasm.

I laughed, but Cinnamon was horrified. I began wondering if she had ever masturbated. She already confessed that she was a virgin. But I assumed sexless people played with themselves more than the rest of us. I certainly did when I was in solitary confinement.

"She's not going to touch herself in the galley, is she?" Cinnamon asked.

Coffee and I replied at the same time saying almost the exact same thing. "I hope not," she said. But I said, "I hope so." My sexy tattooed lover laughed at me, but Cinnamon looked confused.

"Come on, Cinny," I pleaded playfully. "That was funny."

When my favorite spice girl did not reply, Coffee asked her if she masturbated. "I'm not talking about those things with you two," she announced as she urgently jumped out of her chair to sprint from the room.

Before I could follow, Coffee was on my lap, holding my face and kissing my lips. I slid my hands under her shirt to caress her slender body, feeling the slight rise in her skin as her tattoo pulses raced along their circuits. I wasn't sure how much trouble we would get in for fucking on the bridge, but I was willing to risk it. Unfortunately, Coffee stopped the proceedings before it got that far. She giggled at me as she adjusted her clothing and headed toward the galley. I took a moment to adjust my shorts, then gave up on trying to get my growing hard-on to relent. Hopefully, nobody would notice.

I went to join Honeysuckle in the engine room first. I wasn't of much help, but I lingered until the work was done. She was confident that she fixed both problems.

Two hours later we were back in the control room, in the same positions. I sniffed at Strawberry as I leaned over to take the seat beside her. Her fruity scent was strong. I was hoping to smell the distinct aroma of pussy juice on her. Did she really rub one out during the break? Was her statement intended as an invitation? Did she want my company in her quarters?

"Don't be sniffing for my berry juice, dirty boy," Strawberry whispered to me. I was surprised that she not only caught me but actually knew what I was doing. Then she grinned and placed two fingers of her left hand under my nose. I should have been appalled, but of course I wasn't. I took a good whiff but only smelled her signature scent. Was that what her pussy juice smelled like?

Then she laughed at me. "I washed my hands already," she whispered to me with an ornery grin. "If I knew that you were so naughty, I would have saved some for you."

I smiled weakly, not sure how to respond.

"Next time," she told me.

"Definitely," I answered as I tried to regain my confidence.

"Definitely what?" Cinnamon asked from the other side of the control room.

"Definitely shut up!" Sage boomed. "Get professional, please," she said, looking straight to her systems specialist. "If we don't have any failures this time, and we don't shift the wrong way, I'm going to leave the engines on."

"What?" Strawberry asked. This plan was apparently news to her, too.

"We'll go straight to using the thrusters to minimize our risk. Honeysuckle agrees with me."

"Should Kash be in the pilot's chair?" Cinnamon asked looking slightly panicked by the adjustment.

"No!" Sage said. "I can control the thrusters from my seat should the program fail. Which it won't."

I had my reservations about this new plan, simply because it was not announced in advance. Otherwise, it did sound like a good idea not to power down the engines if everything was working well. I just wondered what Sage had up her sleeve with this maneuver. If she sabotaged the ship and killed the two men, could we trust her with our lives?

We waited extra-long for a system failure to pop up, but none did. The computer announced that the vibrations were loosening our grip on the cliff, but that was only more reason to go ahead with powering our ship toward safety.

"Okay, thrusters on!" Sage announced.

I felt a jolt in the ship like a surge sideways, but it stopped quickly. I had learned that there were three thruster jets on each side of the ship for maneuvering in the atmosphere of planets. Pointed laterally the intention was to push us along the ground away from the canyon.

"We only moved one meter," Strawberry announced calmly.

"What is going on, Honeysuckle?" Sage called through the intercom to the mechanic.

"One of the jets failed," Strawberry then said.

"One of the jets failed," Honey's voice repeated through the speaker. "Safety protocol for not being in flight is to shut down the other two so we can isolate the problem. We should delay the maneuver."

"Thirty eight percent," Cinnamon yelled out to get our attention. I could feel the cliff crumbling beneath us, as well as visualize it.

"No!" Sage yelled angrily. "Override the bad jet! I need power now!"

There was no response from Honeysuckle. But a few seconds later the ship rumbled loudly. I knew from my limited experience that the remaining jets fired up again. I felt another surge, but once again our movement ceased. Then the floor tilted toward the canyon. We were going to slip over the edge.

"Two meters that time," Strawberry announced.

"Sixty-two percent!" Cinnamon screamed frantically.

"Fuck!" Coffee yelled. "We're gonna die!"

"No!" Sage yelled as she tapped a couple things on her console. Then she made a motion to increase the acceleration again.

I didn't like this. We were in a perilous situation and it was completely out of my control. If we survived this, I was determined to never be in that position again.

"We're moving!" Strawberry announced. "Three meters! Five meters!"

The ship righted itself causing the bottom hull to make full contact with the surface. The floor vibrated and convulsed as it was being pushed forcibly across debris and uneven terrain.

"What percent now?" Sage demanded to know. Were we sliding across the ground? Or down the side of the cliff? Would the artificial gravity system fool us into thinking that we were upright when we were actually plunging to our doom?

"No reading!" Cinnamon cried out.

"We've gone twelve meters total!" Strawberry cheered. "We're moving in the right direction!"

I let out a heavy sigh and returned to watching the screens. This was a learning experience for me in more ways than one. I needed to capitalize on it.

"Zero percent," Cinnamon called out with obvious relief in her voice.

"Don't go too far," Strawberry told the acting captain.

"How far did we say, Kash?" Sage asked.

"Sixty feet maximum," I replied.

"Twenty meters," Strawberry corrected me. I was using the metric system during all my training, but my brain still thought in old English measurements. "We are approaching that now."

Sage eased off the acceleration and a few seconds later we were at a complete stop. We all cheered. No matter who saved us or who sat and just watched, it felt like a team victory. We were all delighted to be away from the edge of the cliff. Resting on stable ground gave us a lot more options. And a lot more time.

"I'm glad Honeysuckle was able to do the override," I said.

"Yes, me too," Sage replied. Then to the intercom, "Honeysuckle, good job. You did it. We're safe."

I was happy that the often-disrespected mechanic was getting some praise. She deserved it. The slim wisp of a girl had been working harder than any of us to get us ready for this moment. In my mind, she was the biggest hero of the group. I looked forward to telling her so.

The room calmed down quickly when we realized there was no reply from the engine room.

"Honeysuckle?" Sage called again. No response.

CHAPTER SIXTEEN:

"Vanilla!" I heard Sage screaming into the intercom as I darted from the control room. "I need a health status check on Honeysuckle."

I was sprinting past the medical lab as I heard the doctor reply that the mechanic's vitals revealed that she was alive, but unconscious.

I heard footsteps behind me as Sage's voice boomed through the speakers, "I didn't excuse everyone from the bridge yet!"

Cinnamon entered the long hallway as I descended the steps. I heard Coffee calling out from behind her that she was also on her way. Both ignored their leader to check on their friend in the lower level, just like me.

I found Honeysuckle lying on the floor in the engine room, a tool resembling a hex nut driver still clinched in her hand. She was passed out with her legs splayed in my direction, boots on for once. I rushed up to her side and was relieved to find no apparent injuries. No marks on her face or body except for a few black streaks on the hand holding the tool.

"Honey girl," I said to her, hoping to stir her awake. I was tempted to shake her shoulders to get her attention but refrained in case she had internal injuries from falling.

"Don't move her!" Vanilla raised her voice for the first time since I'd known her, other than that time she screamed from seeing Teddy walking around. I was surprised that she arrived the same time as my other girls. But it was a medical emergency, after all.

"I didn't," I replied. "No obvious injuries except for these marks on her..."

"Give me room please," Vanilla asked. "The scanners will tell us everything that we need to know."

I reluctantly backed away and stood beside Coffee and Cinnamon. They were both nervous and concerned over the welfare of their close friend but trusted their medic to give the proper care. They each took one of my hands in theirs, clinching tightly to show how they felt.

"The ship is stable," Strawberry told us over the speaker. "Once the doctor can say the same for Honeysuckle, we have some work to do. Kash, when you are ready, we'll need to check our situation from outside."

"Roger," I replied. I could hear the compassion in Strawberry's voice that was missing from Sage's. She might not have been all that fond of the injured woman, but she had a level of respect for all of us.

"What does that mean?" Strawberry replied.

"Oh," I nearly chuckled. "It's an old term for when we... uh, never mind. I understand. Once Vanilla doesn't need me, I'll get pasted up to go out."

"I'll go with you," Cinnamon said. "If Honey is okay."

"She is," Vanilla said from her position kneeling beside our friend's motionless body. "A power surge knocked her out and has caused some minor damage to her tool hand. I should be able to repair that quickly. She is safe to move now."

Vanilla stepped aside and gestured for us to lift our green skinned friend. I didn't need any help so I did it myself, one arm under her neck and the other below her knees like I would carry her across a threshold after our wedding, should we choose to get married, and follow centuries old traditions. I then wondered if there were anti-grav units specifically for moving unconscious bodies. These girls would struggle to carry me very far, even if three of them worked at it together.

"Oh, my," Vanilla muttered. I wasn't sure if she was impressed with my strength or found the scene romantic.

I shrugged both Cinnamon and Coffee off when they offered to assist. We all rode the lift up to the second level. Then I placed my foxy slumbering white-haired friend in the examination lounge and let Vanilla do her work.

"She'll be fine," Vanilla assured us, taking the time to make eye contact to make us believe. "She'll likely be awake when you return from outside as long as she isn't in too much pain."

"Okay," I replied and gestured that we should get going. After the maneuver of the ship across the land there were all kinds of things that could have gone wrong. Plus, I was genuinely curious at how things looked out there since the move.

"I'm not going outside," Coffee replied stubbornly. She wasn't expected to join us, but it would have been nice to keep the three of us together.

"I need to check on the animals in cargo," Cinnamon announced. Both Coffee and I went with her. I was happy to find none of them seriously injured, especially my little, long-armed alien buddy.

Teddy said, "I just about shit my brand-new pants when the floor tilted. I thought for sure we were going to plunge to our death. Any chance you can let me out of here?"

"Not right now, I'm afraid," I answered apologetically. "I need to go outside and check things over. When things settle down, I'll come back for you."

Cinnamon and I got each other dirtied up quickly from a large batch of the scent blocker that Vanilla had prepared. Outdoor life was about to increase dramatically despite eliminating the threat of falling into the canyon. We decided with our water supply outside the ship and an opportunity to make a secure compound, we should continue with our plans.

Once outside I searched for potential predators quickly, then studied our situation. The hull was moved well clear of the cliff. That was great to see. Large chunks had crumbled and fallen from the ledge due to the vibration of our engines, though. No doubt that was the reason for the brief threat increase during the maneuver.

Our new position placed us at a slightly different angle. The rear of the ship had traveled farther, placing the front at a trajectory roughly fifteen degrees further to the left. Dozens of shrubs and dancing little trees had been plundered by the massive hull, but overall, we appeared to be resting flatter than before. All the debris from the uprooted red tree that was destroyed when the ship first crashed had crumbled under the weight of the Arketa Koreta when it shifted.

Unfortunately, that same bulky tree caused more damage to the exterior along the lower left side. It would likely add days to our repair list getting completed.

Our tail end came to a halt less than forty feet from our cargo where it rested near Gako's home. That was a bit farther than I had planned and meant that we would need to clear away more uneven terrain to give our base a flat floor.

The disruption of our ship powering up and grinding along the planet's surface had caused quite a stir among the local wildlife. One of our mist harvesters had been severely damaged. My guess was that a pair of wofurs or a small herd of laughing red goats trampled through it to get clear of the massive metal bulk headed their way.

All in all, it was still a great success. The only significant negative was Honeysuckle's injury. But I believed Vanilla when she told me that it was a minor wound and should be easily healed.

"Kash?" Strawberry's voice came through my wrist communicator. "Major systems check good in here. We have a few issues to add to our repair list, but it won't interfere with your plans out there."

"Thanks," I told her. "There is some damage to the front and left side hull, too. Otherwise, everything out here looks fine. Should we start moving the cubes?"

"No," Sage's voice entered the conversation. She sounded angry that her first officer and I were getting along so well professionally. "We need to meet to discuss first, adjusting for any new circumstances. I don't want to be left out of the loop."

I took video of the area from the ground level and from the top of the nearest hull ladder. I had learned how to use the ship's computer to quickly convert the data to a topographical map. That would help us immensely with our plans.

I had no interest in rushing back into the ship to wait for Sage to grace us with her presence. If she wanted an update, she could call me once she was ready. Instead, I started marking the ground where we would be moving the mist harvesters and the cargo containers. It would leave us fifteen feet of open space between the large L-shape that would provide a measure of security, and the hull of the ship. We had enough heavy-duty fabric among the stored goods to make a sloped roof to block us from the eyes of predators.

My excitement was contagious. I could see it in Cinnamon's gorgeous brown eyes. She had never built anything before. Not many people did in this day and age, she explained.

As children, the people living on space stations learned basic skills and how to become a useful part of society. At age sixteen or seventeen they chose a field of employment to pursue. Most jobs required just one to three years of courses to become proficient. Test scores and personality classifications were public knowledge available to any employer. Job hunting no longer existed.

The data and search engines did all the work. Upon completion of your courses, or sometimes even before that, your information would rank you for potential employers. Job offers would appear in your messages with descriptions and salary bids. You simply clicked to accept a position and showed up for work at the designated time and place.

Not getting any good offers? Well, you should have put a little more effort into your test scores. Or as was the case just as often, not be such an asshole to others.

The system discouraged people from alienating others by their behavior. Don't like skinny chicks? Keep it to yourself. At least until you found a secure job. Even then, though, you could be terminated for personality issues. To avoid that you would need to find employment on a small ship and become indispensable.

Did I just join a crew of pent-up misfits? Maybe, but they were all as sexy as a naughty princess in a schoolgirl outfit. Besides, I didn't have any options at this point. These six women were my world, and probably would be for a while. If I didn't get myself killed.

All of us, everyone except the injured Honeysuckle, met in the galley to address the array of negative results after moving the ship. The list was more extensive than I had imagined. But once that was done, we moved on to the base building plans. With repairs required to make the ship ready for interstellar flight expected to take weeks, my proposed base had become a priority.

"Congratulations, Kash," Strawberry said to me after the meeting. "All you do is win, win, win."

"Excuse me?" Was she quoting a song from my day?

"You won over half the crew without much of a battle. You killed a dragon to save your own life, then befriended another. You are obviously training an intelligent alien to be one of your followers. And now you are getting your own domain outside the ship. A place that will not fall under my direct control."

"Oh, well it is not really about that," I told her. And for the most part that was true.

"I forgot to mention how you won me over, too."

"Yeah?" I replied with unconcealed delight. Those were some especially important words to hear, but I certainly didn't expect them.

"When you saved my sexy ass from going over the cliff," she whispered as she pulled me close. Her strong scent of Strawberries was a natural aphrodisiac that was disorienting all on its own. Add her crazy attractive freckled redhead sex doll appearance, and I was practically under her spell.

"Don't you think so?" she asked with heavy breath on my neck. She was getting seductively close.

"Yes," I replied without understanding the question. "I mean, what?"

"My ass," Strawberry answered as she stared into my eyes. "Don't you think that it is sexy?"

Absolutely! Her ass was exquisite, definitely one of her best features. But should I tell her that? We hadn't even left the galley yet. I knew that they others were still in the room, somewhere behind her full head of crimson hair.

"Enough already," Cinnamon told her as she slid her arm through mine like we were a couple. Were we a couple? Maybe kind of, sort of, but not really. "We have work to do."

Strawberry adjusted to my best friend's announced presence smoothly. She had some skills that must have made her a key asset in negotiations with suppliers and buyers.

"Yes, we do," she replied to Cinnamon. "And I look forward to working more with both of you."

"More?" Cinny asked. "We'll be spending half our time outside now."

"Yes," Seductive berry girl answered. "And I'll be joining you as much as I can." She then allowed a pause for effect, or maybe for us to reply with confusion. "As one of Kash's girls, of course."

Then she turned and walked away without a backwards glance.

"What was that about?" Coffee asked as she approached.

Cinnamon frowned, looking genuinely concerned. Then she answered, "We have competition."

CHAPTER SEVENTEEN:

I had to admit, I was more than a little worried when I first opened the exit door. The two of us were pasted up good, so I wasn't concerned about dragons. This time joining Cinnamon and me, was Teddy. It would be his first legitimate shot at escaping, if he should be so inclined.

My favorite spice girl carried the pistol in its proper holster on her lovely hip. Instead of opting for the rifle, as I had every right to do these days, I grabbed the electro-gun that we had claimed from the weapons cargo. If my little alien buddy decided to run off, I planned to shock the shit out of him. I certainly didn't want to shoot him with the bolt pistol or the energy rifle. Killing him would be worse than letting him escape.

He stepped out onto the crushed grass surface between the huge engines like it was no big deal. Of course, he wasn't stupid enough to run for it right away. A smart guy like him would wait for a chance when he had his best opportunity to succeed.

Teddy took a moment to test the ground with his fuzzy orange feet. The bottom of each had black padded sections like an animal from Earth. Shoes were beyond our limited ability anyway, so he would need to remain barefoot. I gave him the heads up on things he should avoid stepping on. If he could manage to stay out of the taller grass, he should be fine if he watched where he stepped.

The loader came out right behind us. I'm not going to lie. The massive robot following me put some pep in my step. Even though I knew that Cinnamon had it fully under her control. I just felt like I was about to get pulverized by a warrior mech from one of my favorite video games as a child.

I rounded the corner first and studied the ground, trees and air for threats. Then I sniffed the air.

"I smell something weird," Teddy said. He puckered up his lips like he wanted a kiss, but I think it was a natural byproduct of him wrinkling his nose.

"Everything smells weird on this planet," Cinnamon replied.

"You are not wrong about that, miss," Teddy responded to her comment, nearly choking on the last word. His species had a society that was very male dominant. It wasn't until our agreement that he began speaking to human females. Showing proper respect was a tad challenging for him, but I was happy with his effort.

Once he got a full view of the world around him, Teddy surprised me. He had always come across as guarded and angry. I expected him to simply nod at his surroundings and continue on his surly way. Instead, the effect on him was profound.

He blinked his large dark orange eyelids several times as if holding off tears. Then his face trembled like he was holding back a sneeze. Initially, I thought he was just having a reaction to the bright green sky and the strange aroma in the air. It wasn't until his knees quivered and he fell forward onto his hands that I got concerned.

"Are you okay?" Cinnamon asked as she rushed toward him.

Teddy immediately raised his hand up in her direction, palm forward. "Stay back!" he cried out emotionally.

"Let me help you," my girl said with a tone of genuine concern. Even though he had offered her nothing but rudeness until recently, she was quick to come to his aid.

"Turn around!" Teddy then screeched out.

"Why?" Cinnamon asked as she knelt down beside the traumatized alien monkey.

His hand dropped to the ground to help keep him from falling face forward into the grass. Drooping his head, he began to sob. "Please," he begged her.

"Give him space," I told her. "Turn around like he asked. Give him some privacy, Cinnamon."

She was clearly concerned about my little friend and reluctant to leave him be. When I gave her those instructions, she suddenly realized what was going on and backed up before turning sideways. Teddy was caught in an emotionally vulnerable moment by a female of another species. In his society, it was the equivalent of being put on display naked in town square for everyone to laugh at.

"Thank you, Kash," Teddy muttered as he struggled to regain his composure.

"No problem, dude," I answered. I knew about humiliation, and the deep pain that could come with it. We didn't want that feeling to linger.

"No," he responded as he raised his big black eyes toward me. "Thank you for bringing me outside, even if it is just for a brief walk. I spent weeks in that cage thinking that I would never again step foot on a planet's surface. I knew that I would be sold to someone living in one of those metal contraptions in the night sky. A human station. My kind were not meant for the indoors."

"I'm so sorry, Teddy," Cinnamon said as she cautiously took a step toward him.

"You stay over there," he commanded her, sounding much more like his disgruntled self. Then a bit softer, "Please. This is difficult for me."

"Dude," I said. "I'm incredibly happy for you. I'm glad to see you enjoying the outdoors. But Cinnamon is not a Pythynos female."

"She and your other women will be laughing at me tonight," he replied. "While I am stuck again in my dungeon."

"We will not!" Cinnamon sounded appalled because she interpreted the situation as an opportunity to comfort him.

His hand went back up firmly telling her to stop. "Kash, tell her not to patronize me."

"I honestly don't think that she is," I told him as I stepped slowly toward him. "I don't believe anyone will be laughing over this. They might be ooing and awing about how cute it is..."

"That's worse," Teddy mumbled, then coughed like he might vomit.

"Then we won't tell them," I said. He glanced at Cinnamon to see her reaction to my statement. "Or we will at least downplay it. Stop worrying about it, Teddy. You should be enjoying yourself while you are out here, not stressing over what other people think."

Teddy perked up a little but kept looking Cinnamon's way to see if she was about to burst out laughing. The scene was comical to me, but I knew that she wouldn't hurt him that way. My girl was a good person through and through.

"Cinny," I said with an up tone that marked the beginning of a new conversation. "Why don't you go ahead and get the loader working on moving those cargo units. Teddy and I will start marking the ground for the sections where we'll put some empty ones on their side. We'll make a few tiny little rooms for us."

The little guy followed me like a toddler in the park, happy just to be alive. Despite his typical grumpy nature, he was lifting my spirits merely by his presence.

"So, what kind of conversations do you have with your cellmates?"

"Cellmates?" Teddy asked. "Oh, the two beasts with which I must share my unfortunate domicile. Not much, really. They tell me they are hungry and anxious, or even horny. And I tell them to shut the fuck up."

"That's it?" I chuckled. "Have you ever told them to do anything else? Like a command that could help me appreciate that they are trainable, possibly usable for the cause."

"I have a few times," Teddy admitted. "But I am not the one that feeds them, so I mostly get a blank stare. Perhaps if you worked on your grunts and purrs you could command them as will." He was going back to being a bit of an asshole.

"Perhaps," I replied as I drug the heel of my boot through the dirt to mark spots for cargo cubes. The first one was already on its way as Cinnamon carefully navigated the uneven terrain with the controller. "Or I could let you start feeding them. Can I trust you to properly convey my wishes to them?"

"Of course, Kash," he answered readily, snapping out of his funk. "The way I see it, as no doubt you do as well, you are my ticket out of this mess. You give me liberties, an envious amount of freedom for a caged pet, and I will follow your instructions impeccably. The more power that you gain, the better chance I have of achieving real freedom. Though you have not briefed me on your ambitions, I have picked up on as much crew gossip as I can. I am certain that you will find me to be a loyal and valuable follower."

"Really?" I asked as I came to a sudden halt. Either his species liked to be right up front with how they feel, or he thought that I was an idiot to be played. I might as well test both theories. "What kind of things can you do?"

"My arms are stronger than they appear," Teddy replied. "I can crush a human windpipe with my hands."

I got past the shock of the statement and decided on a humorous reply. "Are you saying that you could choke a bitch if I wanted you to?"

"Yes. A bitch. I could choke it," Teddy stumbled through his reply. I got the feeling that he didn't fully understand. "I can also manipulate many of your weapons. A gun, should it not be heavy enough to tip me over."

I laughed outright catching Cinnamon's attention. I waved her off. She didn't need to know this stuff.

"Can you climb that ladder on the hull of the ship?" I asked.

Teddy turned to check it out. "Yes, probably faster than you."

"With those orangutan arms of yours," I said. "No offense. But I'm betting that you can climb trees pretty well."

"Kash, my people make their homes in trees."

I nodded as I thought about the situation, and the unexpected exchange of information. If Teddy could Doctor Doolittle, climb trees, shoot guns and choke bitches, why would he need me?

"Why follow me then?" I asked. "Why not run off right now and make a new life for yourself."

Teddy approached slowly. He apparently did not want to be overheard. The noise of the loader was not enough to completely drown out our conversation and Cinnamon was not far away. He didn't trust her yet, and maybe he never would. I hoped I was reading that issue clearly, that it was just because she was female. Not that he overheard her plotting against me.

"This is not my home. Though considerably better than the cage, it is not worth trying to escape. I may well end up as food for one of these dragons that you talk about. Besides, that is not my style. My people do contracts. Like short term jobs."

"I know what a contract is."

"Good," he answered. "I would like to make one with you. You have my unwavering support for a full galactic year. In return, you make sure that I am promptly returned to my home immediately after. To be clear, though, this is not sexual in nature. It is important to clarify that I will not have sex with you or anyone else at your command. Except maybe the doctor, though I'm not sure how that would work."

"Yeah, I saw you eyeballing Vanilla," I answered. "Okay. No sex for sure. Nobody wants that tiny dick of yours anyway."

I took a chance on the insult to judge his response. People liked to make huge boasts about their dedication, then when they hit a tiny snag it is all over.

Teddy said nothing for a moment. He looked like he might be getting angry, but it was difficult to tell. Finally, he responded, "they shall not have it regardless."

I laughed at how well he brushed it off. I did not know a single human male that wouldn't at least flinch at an insult regarding his penis. Or his mother. Should I try insulting his mama?

"Deal," I told him with my hand extended. He stared at it for just a couple seconds before realizing that he needed to put his hand in mine. His palm was leathery, and his grip was firm. His offer to strangle someone had merit, though I sincerely hoped that it would not come to that.

"You will follow commands from others that I designate?"

"Unless I believe they contradict with your will."

"What are you guys doing over here?" Cinnamon asked as she walked up. The loader stopped roughly ten feet behind her waiting for its next command.

I ignored her question and turned my attention back to Teddy. "Climb the loader and sit on its head," I commanded him.

Without hesitation Teddy ran to the loader, ape style using his fists like a front pair of feet. He scrambled up the dormant mechanical monster quickly, having no difficulty finding hand holds along the way. He plopped his ass on top of its head and looked down at me without a word.

"Wow," Cinnamon said as she watched. "Do I continue moving containers with him up there?"

"You can if you want..." I started to say.

"What is that smell?" Teddy interrupted me just before shadows raced across the ground. Looking up I spotted three black dragons approaching. Teddy scrambled back down to the ground as quick as he could. "Mother of shit!"

I had never heard that curse before, but I shared its sentiment. Fortunately, the dragons passed by without attacking. Then they landed on the top of the hull before turning to face us like vultures waiting for their chance.

I regretted not having the pistol. I was about to ask for it when I saw that Cinnamon was too busy manipulating the loader to take a position between us and the dragons. Could she fight them with that thing?

CHAPTER EIGHTEEN:

The black dragons rested intimidatingly on the edge of the ship's hull, staring down at us. Their skinny necks moved back and forth like a drunk gangster trying to give us attitude. Red eyes and bared teeth made them appear even more menacing from their advantageous high ground position.

I took the electro pistol in my left hand, holding it steady in their direction as I used my right to get my sword ready for action. Hopefully, we appeared to be formidable opponents and they would rethink attacking us. Scaring them off the top of the ship would be another matter entirely. Shots would need to be fired, which could in turn encourage an attack.

I didn't bother to look around for Gako. He hadn't been spotted since he declared his desire to go searching for his wife. I would love to have his support at this moment.

Of course, Teddy was anything but intimidating. I half expected him to cling to my leg like a toddler. Instead, he stood there frozen, in fear I presumed at first.

"Kash," he then said to me calmly. "What would you like for me to do?"

"Don't get eaten," I replied instinctively.

"I will certainly do my best. Anything else perhaps?"

He was taking in this situation much better than I had anticipated. If we all survived this encounter, I was looking forward to grooming him for a regular sidekick position.

"Yes," I told him. "Move slowly over to Cinnamon and get the pistol from her. Then bring it to me."

"Kash?" my girl said with obvious doubt in her voice. Handing a weapon to a prisoner was a definite no-no. "Is that a good idea?"

"Self-preservation will assure that he doesn't do anything against us," I told her.

Teddy didn't say a word. He just made his way carefully to Cinnamon's position, stopping only one time due to a loud cry from the middle dragon. Once he retrieved the pistol, he promptly brought it to me.

"Take this thing," I told him, gesturing with the electrogun. I only had two hands, and it was only right to let him protect himself, even if it was with the weakest weapon available. His fingers manipulated the firearm as well as a human.

I wasn't much of a shot left-handed. But I was probably even worse using it to swing the sword, so I stayed as I was.

"It appears to be a stalemate," Teddy said, remaining calmer than I felt. "Should we instigate to control this conflict?"

I liked where his head was at. I learned as a kid getting into scrapes in the neighborhood that it was usually better to be proactive than reactive, especially if my opponent appeared to have the upper hand.

"If we wait," Cinnamon responded, a measure of fear evident in her high-pitched voice. "We may get reinforcements from inside. Your new girlfriend has the rifle."

She was of course referring to Strawberry. There was definitely some jealousy in her tone, too. But her mention of reinforcements got me thinking. What were the dragons waiting for? Were they thinking just like Cinnamon?

A slight breeze was coming from behind me. Very slight, but it was enough to carry the scent of freshly cut cucumbers. That was the same smell that Teddy whiffed from atop the loader when the three black dragons arrived.

"Oh, no!" Teddy said, turning to look behind us the same time as me. Two more dragons landed on the ground not more than thirty feet away.

The sound of loader joint whirring brought my attention back to front and center. The left stinky lizard from on top of the hull had swooped directly for me. A massive metal arm of the loader shifted to block its path. So, the ugly thing tried to bite the mechanical device instead.

The first thing I thought about that was that Sage was not going to be happy if the loader took damage. In fact, she might prefer that the mechanical cargo shifter was the only one on our side to come out of this intact.

The fight was more than a dozen feet in front of me, too far for the sword. Instead, I fired a shot left-handed into the beast's crotch, though I was shooting for its chest. My aim was off because I was overly concerned about striking the loader instead. Though not death dealing by any imagination, it was enough to annoy the dragon to the point that it released its toothy grip on the metal arm. Cinn then spun the upper half like a warrior mech to punch the fucker in the back of the head. He hit the ground hard but scrambled away on its feet before realigning its wings for flight.

The dragon on the right up top flew around to attack Cinnamon. She dove to the ground while still holding the controller, giving me plenty of room for error with the pistol. This time I put three holes in a bat-like dragon wing, just inches apart from each other. It wasn't enough to stop the attack.

I ran forward and swung my blade before the creature could get its teeth into my sweet spice girl. It couldn't pull its head back fast enough. I put a nice nick in its neck to draw an instant squirt of blood.

I heard the distinct sound of the electrogun then, right behind me. Teddy shocked the shit out of one of the flanking dragons that was coming at me from the rear. It was stunned and irritated enough by the injury to retreat. But its partner was right behind him targeting Teddy. I placed two shots in the thing's ass just as another pulse of electricity erupted from Teddy's weapon. The beast's right wing convulsed wildly throwing it backwards.

Cinnamon got back to her feet as I swirled around in search of the next attacker. Only the middle dragon that cried out earlier had remained on its perch, observing. It must be the leader, I assumed. It stared intently at me alone as the other four took up positions to encircle us.

"They have learned our weapons," Teddy told me as he backed his way toward us. "They will adjust their strategy on the next attack to compensate. I would not expect us to handle the upcoming round as competently."

"Can you make the loader charge?" I asked Cinnamon.

"Not super-fast, but yeah. Which one do I charge?"

"Start at the one directly in front of you, then adjust to hit the one on your right instead. Can you do that?"

"I think so," she replied, but not with much confidence. Surely controlling a loader in battle had not been part of her training.

"Shall I do the same?" Teddy asked, lowering his voice. I hadn't taken into consideration that the dragons could understand our speech.

"No," I chuckled. "I doubt that they will find you as intimidating as the mech."

"What if I..." Teddy started to say when the next organized attack came.

All four dragons on the ground pounced at once. Only the leader remained out of play to observe. Cinnamon did just as I asked. The first target backed up to rethink things as the other charged her back. The loader rotated smoothly and swung its arms with great force toward the second attacker as my girl calmly stepped past it while dipping her head.

I fired several bolts at the one charging me from the front while turning to swing my blade behind me. I cut off a dragon's right arm with the sharp blade. Surprisingly, none of them were targeting my little buddy. So, he was free to choose.

Realizing that the bolt pistol had a better chance at protecting me than the sword, Teddy shot a lightning bolt out of the barrel of his gun to strike my rear attacker in the eye. What a sight! Black blood gushing from its severed arm and a wide mouthed gator face being lit up like a holiday tree. But I didn't have time to truly admire it.

The dragon in front of me only flinched from acquiring its wing holes. None of my shots hit bone or even thick cartilage. It continued forward and nearly had its jowls around my head by the time I thrust upward with the tip of my sword. The thin blade pierced the soft skin under its mouth and kept on going until it exited through the thing's right eyeball.

I pried my weapon back out before it fell lifeless to the ground, nearly on top of me. Instinctively I pressed the green button to clean the blade, surprising myself with my clear thinking.

I whirled around to face the next biggest threat to our survival. The three attacking dragons that remained all retreated once again. Their leader then casually dropped to the ground from its perch on top of the ship to take the dead dragon's place. Perhaps they practiced all their maneuvers with four, like a squad on a sports team.

It was the first time that I noticed the new addition to the attacking force was thirty percent larger than the others. It also had several scars on its face and along its belly. An experienced war veteran, evidently.

They began to circle us counterclockwise. The maneuver made us switch our targets as they went. It was a good tactical procedure, like forcing a defense to drop out of man coverage. These dragons were smart. Just like my friend Gako. Could they communicate as clearly as him?

"Can you negotiate with these dragons?" I asked Teddy.

"They are oozing hatred, but I can try," he responded. Then he spoke to the leader. "Any chance that we can talk about this?" he asked the big black dragon.

"Well, I could have done that," I muttered.

"Your dragon speaks Galactic Standard," Teddy retorted. "Why wouldn't these?"

I suddenly remembered the black dragons that tried to get at me and the three girls in the brittle dancing trees when we were retrieving water. They did sound like they were speaking English, only just one word at a time.

"Die!" the leader screamed, confirming Teddy's assumption. Then they pounced again.

The big fella flew upwards and shoved its two rear feet at the head of the loader, kangaroo style. It tumbled backwards and nearly crushed Cinnamon as she had to dive to the side to avoid it. I fired two more shots at the nearest predator in front of me and swung my blade backwards again. This time there was no one there. They had learned that technique already.

Instead, one of the rear dragons propelled itself forward quickly using its wings to straddle Cinnamon as she laid face down on the ground. I fired three shots at its head from close range. It didn't explode like I had hoped, but it did wobble and fall over, only scratching one of my girl's sexy legs with the large talon of a rear foot.

The remaining attacked, ignored Teddy once again, and managed to dodge his electric shock as it ran toward me with its wings pulled back. I turned just in time to see down its throat. I brought my sword up quickly, but it was going to be too late. The beast nearly had my head in its front teeth already.

A ball of energy then struck its neck and continued on through. The beast stopped short and snapped its teeth together loudly. Staring at me from inches away it was confused on where the shot had come from. Then a second pulse bored through its chest from one side to the other. The shots came from our lone rifle.

Strawberry was down on one knee and using the other to steady the weapon, sniping my would-be killer from a hundred feet away.

Three dragons down. If not dead, they were currently disabled. Rebounding from those injuries might be possible, for some of these intimidating creatures. I had no idea. From the look of the leader, though, he was not yet ready to concede.

We had already revealed all of our tricks and the loader was not currently operational. I had forgotten how many shots I had fired, or even how many the pistol held. I could be out of ammo already. If so, we were down to just two close range weapons.

The largest dragon took note of Strawberry's appearance on the scene and quickly orchestrated a shift to place us between the remaining two and our powerful rifle. I had to step over Cinnamon to keep her from being the first line of defense. She had managed to pull her cutter from its sheath but was still prone in the grass.

Teddy slung himself up the frame of the toppled loader like a monkey to rest as high as possible, tossing the limited use weapon between his hands like a juggler as he climbed. His acrobatics would have been quite a show to watch if it weren't for our predicament.

Big black, red-eyed, sharp-toothed mother fucker screamed again, then took flight toward my face. But he missed. By a lot. In fact, he just kept going upward. It wasn't until I turned to watch him from behind that I saw the green scales of a larger dragon. Gako had returned and came to my rescue once again.

That still left one dragon to account for. It was trying to sneak around me to bite at Cinnamon's wounded leg. Before I could swing my blade to protect her another large green dragon appeared on the scene and knocked the smaller black on its side. One foot pinning the thing to the ground, the green dragon sat on the rest of its body to demobilize it. It also looked like Gako.

Then it spoke. I couldn't be sure by the tone, but the words lead me to believe that this second one must be Gako's wife, lover or female companion. He hadn't gotten into details.

"You must be Cinnamon," the friendly beast said looking down at my girl.

Cinnamon scrambled to her knees and seemed to just realize that she had a nasty scratch on one leg.

"Off!" the black dragon that was pinned to the ground yelled.

Gako's big girlfriend reacted by biting clean through the animal's neck, nearly severing its head. The squirming stopped immediately.

CHAPTER NINETEEN:

I knew that things and people tended to look alike if you were not familiar with them. If you had never encountered African Americans or Asian Americans before, they might all look remarkably similar. It could be hard to tell them apart.

The same was true of music. If you had no experience with classical, reggae or blue grass music, you might have a real difficult time distinguishing between the individual pieces within their genre. It didn't mean that you were prejudice. You simply had not been familiar.

This mentality certainly applied to dragons on an alien planet.

Those of different colors were easy enough to sort out. But within each color, each dragon race, it was hard to tell them apart unless they were of significantly different size.

That was the case when Gako and his mate first took a position side-by-side in front of us. However, as we began to converse, I could clearly see what made the female unique. A narrower nose. Larger eyes and lips. I bigger butt. Even her voice had a more distinct female tone. She also spoke at least twice the speed of her companion. That helped move the conversation along.

"I like you," Dawynda said to Cinnamon as she rested her head on the ground beside my best friend. "Do you like dragons?"

Cinnamon was not at all comfortable with the giant lizard's presence, but she was doing her best to tolerate it. "Not usually," Cinnamon replied.

"I want you to like me," Dawynda told her, acting like a teenage girl in front of her favorite pop music star. "The way that I like you. How do I make that happen?"

"Don't eat me," my friend cringed as she answered, pulling her wounded leg closer.

"I can agree to that," the female dragon responded quickly. "Maybe some licking, after we get to know each other. What else? Surely you need more in order to warm up to me. I can see that you are uncomfortable with me this close, and I want to change that. How do I do it?"

"I don't know," Cinnamon answered, simply bewildered that a dragon was saying such things to her. "Why do you like me?"

"It's the smell," Teddy muttered from nearby.

"You do smell good," Dawynda answered. "But you also have heart, and integrity. And you have gained a self-sacrificing love from your man. These are all admirable qualities in a human. Yet, I think it might be your eyes that tell me who you are. Why don't you try touching me?"

"What?"

"Place your hand on my scales. Touch my neck, my back, my belly. I want you to get familiar with me."

"How come you and I never had this conversation?" I asked Gako as Dawynda shifted position to give Cinnamon access to more parts of her body.

Gako snorted fiercely, hot air bursting from his nostrils. I took it as laughter.

"Only women say those things. They find something or someone and become fixated on them," Gako told me. "Since I've known Dawynda she has bonded to a chattler, a blue bird, and a tree snake."

"What is a chattler?" I asked.

"They are all dead now, so it doesn't matter," Gako replied. "Dawynda tried to save the species but they were too few to begin with. Plus, they tasted really good to eat."

I looked back to see Cinnamon petting her reptilian friend on the neck and upper belly. She was clearly getting more comfortable with her quickly.

"I kind of feel like I'm not needed here," Strawberry said in a very uncharacteristic tone. She was a confident woman but completely out of her element.

With Cinnamon engaged with her new dragon friend and no one else around, except Teddy, I decided this was a good opportunity for me. I stepped over to Strawberry and slid my arm around her narrow waist. Resting that hand on her hip I found her body to be very firm.

"I really appreciate you coming to our rescue," I told her.

"You are welcome," she replied with a grin as she placed her free hand on my back. The other hand was still holding the rifle in the direction of the two green dragons. She had never befriended one before, so she was more than wary.

I caught her staring at my lips. Was she really considering kissing me?

"It is impressive," she said before I could make a move, her eyes looking almost as dreamy as Dawynda's.

"What is?"

"You have managed to win over practically the entire crew, two dragons, and a fuzzy orange alien. Of course, being male gave you some advantages. But it also made it more challenging. Men are not easy to trust in our world. I certainly had my doubts."

Was I becoming the good guy for the first time in my life? Could I actually be making my mama proud for once?

"And now?" I asked.

"I'm ready," she replied.

"Ready for what?"

"I'm ready to jump on the Kash express ship," she replied. "Only, I have some demands."

"Demands?" I asked, raising one eyebrow like my favorite wrestler.

"Let's call them prerequisites," she answered. "My loyalty to you is secret until the right time. It is imperative that Sage does not feel abandoned. She will not respond well if she does."

"Okay."

"I will not be your bottom girl," she then said. "Honestly, I should be your top. But I can see how fond you are of Cinnamon. Perhaps I can be on the other arm as an equal."

"Yeah?"

"Surely you see more value in me than Honeysuckle or Coffee."

She had a point. As much as I had grown fond of the two weaker women, they were not near as big of assets as her. It was a no brainer to promise her whatever she wanted to get her allegiance. I was just a bit concerned about this issue between her and Honey.

"I do."

"Good," she said. "I have one more demand. This one is essential to our alliance."

"Okay, what is it?"

"You must fuck me, Kash."

Woah! My mind sounded like the noise from one of the wofurs. Of course, I was not against the idea. "Right here?" I asked. "Right now? In front of the others?"

Strawberry laughed hard. I had not seen her do that before. It was fun to watch as she struggled to control her composure.

"No, Kash," she finally answered. "Not right now. But soon. And your other women must know about it."

Hmmm. I kind of understood where she was going with this. "Should they watch?" I asked.

This time just a wide grin. "That is up to you," she said softly. "I just want my position to be known among your followers."

Her position. I would have to give this some thought. Bringing Strawberry to the cause was worth some sacrifices, for sure. But I didn't want to get played. I couldn't just give her dominance over Coffee and Strawberry, as if they would even accept it. But some of this could be worked out after the sex.
I let my hand slide down her hip to rest on the upper portion of her firm ass cheek. The I remembered what she had said. It wasn't until now that she fully trusted me. I needed to be careful what I promised if I didn't want her to eventually turn against me. A woman scorned is…

"Is it okay for me to pee on the ground in front of you," Teddy then asked from nearby. "Or should I go back inside.

I had been distracted. I glanced back to see Cinnamon conversing with her new best friend, Dawynda. Gako looked like he was taking a nap after devouring half of one of the dead dragons. There were no other threats at the present. Teddy had nothing to do except feel the pressure of his bladder.

In that moment, a new reality set in. I thought I had been focused before, but I was wrong. Things were happening much faster than I expected. My realm of influence was growing exponentially. I needed to handle it responsibly.

Here is what I came up with at that defined moment. I was taking over this shit. All of it. But I had to be smart.

I had a dragon friend. But Cinnamon's giant lizard seemed even more attached to her. I was already giving that girl priority. Now I needed to for power reasons. She would be my top woman, my regular bed companion, my queen.

Strawberry was jumping on board and I needed to handle that delicately so that she received all the respect that she deserved while I avoided disrespecting Coffee and Honeysuckle. That was going to be challenging. However, with my berry flavored new girl wanting a slow and smooth transition, I had time to gradually bring her into the fold.

Teddy was worthy of his freedom. He had ample opportunity to flee during the battle. Instead, he put himself in harm's way. There was no longer a reason to worry about him. I passionately believed that the more freedom I gave him the closer he would follow me. As he himself said, I am his ticket to real freedom.

However, this web that I was constructing could fall apart on me at any moment. Gako and his wife could turn sour and decide we'd make better food than friends. I could reveal my plans to Strawberry, and she'd go straight back to Sage with that information. Teddy could run off and cost me points with the entire crew. And with my mouth, I could easily say the wrong thing and put any particular woman on the warpath against me. This sudden realization helped me keep my ego in check, which hadn't always been easy to do back on Earth.

My tendency in the past was to get a big head when things were going my way. I always bragged when I was winning at poker. I thought that I was the ultimate player when I scored the hottest woman at the club, regardless of how small the establishment or crowd was. I had a reputation of being a bad winner and a sore loser. Where did that get me? In prison. On death row even.

Personal growth was actually much more likely when things weren't going my way. Yet the best time to correct your personality flaws was when you had huge opportunities before you. I was so focused on doing what needed done that I was even prepared to swear off sex for a couple weeks, if needed. Of course, that wouldn't work since I promised to bed Strawberry to gain her allegiance. Or at least she claims that is a requirement.

I wondered if she had those cute Raggedy Ann freckles on her ass, too.

CHAPTER TWENTY:

The loader had sustained some damage. Cinnamon and Honeysuckle worked together to get it operational as fast as possible so we could continue setting up our outdoor base. During that time, I tried to strengthen my relationship with Gako. It would be great to have him as attached to me as his female was to Cinny.

Dragons were the worst racists in the galaxy is what I learned. They each hated all the other colors, some more than others. Hilariously, each type of dragon had certain characteristics for which they were slurred commonly. Green dragons slept too much. Black dragons were stupid. Orange dragons were the worst lovers. I didn't want to picture that mentally. Yellow dragons were childish and blue dragons thought they were God's gift to dragonhood.

Only the red dragons weren't made fun of publicly. As the largest of the species, they apparently drew more respect than the others. We were fortunate that none lived or hunted in our particular area.

Some of the races were more organized than others. No governments per se, but there were a few rules. Mostly about respecting territories and hunting rights. In that regard it seemed that the smaller the dragon the more responsible that they had to be. That made since, I guessed.

Gako and Dawynda were greens which were some of the largest of their type. It would be frowned upon if they relocated to where other green dragons were, but other than that they didn't really have many restrictions. They could eat and sleep where they wanted. Though not entirely monogamous, they tended to pair up and remain somewhat attached to their partner for the rest of their lives.

I talked about the world where I had lived and the adjustments I had to make since my arrival. Not just because of the alien planet, but also due to humankind advancing and changing since my time. I could feel my bond with Gako growing as we continued to converse. Yet it was still nothing compared to Dawynda's fondness for Cinnamon. I was beginning to get jealous. The female alien reptile was resting her chin on my girl's shoulder!

Could you imagine that? A criminal with a death sentence gets sent to another world where he has varied sexual relationships with multiple beautiful women. Then he gets jealous over one of them getting close to a dragon. It was ridiculous, but I could feel the discomfort churning inside me. I decided to direct my thoughts more toward the avenues where I had some control instead.

Strawberry went back inside, naturally. With Gako and Dawynda protecting Cinnamon and Teddy I walked with her to the entrance. That gave us some privacy. Before she opened the door to the ship, I pulled her to me, both arms firmly around her narrow waist, and kissed her on those rosy red lips. She seemed happy to receive my affection. I was tempted to take it farther, but I needed to be cautious. If I let my hormones take control, I would be more likely to make mistakes. And my plan was delicate to say the least.

Once the loader was repaired, we went back about our business of setting up our outdoor base. Gako rested comfortably in his tree watching, but Dawynda did her best to assist in the process of moving the crates. Cinnamon got frustrated with her a few times and I was shocked to see the huge green dragon apologetic. That beast had it bad for my girl. That just made me want to keep Cinnamon as close as possible.

Teddy wasn't worth a shit when it came to moving stuff. Though his arms were strong for his size, he was pathetically small. At least he was smart enough to know his limitations. The only time that his assistance came in handy was when we needed to hook the roof canopy to the ship. He was as agile as an Earth monkey when it came to climbing.

Once the base was set up, we harvested water from the mist trappers and carried it inside. Honeysuckle had a list of repairs a mile long and the two of us teamed up on a few that we could handle to knock them out quickly. Honey looked a little concerned over my determination to stay paired up with Cinnamon as we worked, but due to recent developments I felt that it was essential.

Teddy hung out with us for a while, but there wasn't much that he could do. I urged him to help Honeysuckle in any way he could, like handing her tools and parts, and I was happy that he obliged. Honey even said that his assistance was a real asset.

Once the outdoor work was done it was already dinner time. I talked Cinnamon into sharing a shower stall with me as we cleaned the scent blocking mud off our bodies.

"We're just getting clean, right?" she asked.

"Yes," I snickered. "I won't try anything, I promise."

She took off her uniform bashfully and tossed it into the laundry chute with one arm across her breasts and her thighs pinched together. Her leg injury was minor and healed almost immediately from treatment. Her light brown skin was so gorgeous and her body lines exquisite. I couldn't take my eyes off her as I also disrobed.

"Why are you so shy?" I asked. It was such a dramatic difference from the other girls on the ship. My brain had been associating their sexually assertive personalities with the future.

"You know why," she answered. Ah yes, her virginity.

"Just because you are a virgin doesn't mean that you have to hide your body," I explained. "I promised to be a gentleman. You are so smoking hot that you surely can't be worried about your appearance."

"Thanks, Kash," she blushed. "But I don't think that it works that way. At least not for me."

As we were washing up, I asked her to scrub my back for me. I was happy when she allowed me to return the favor. It took a lot of self-control, more than I thought that I had, to keep from caressing and fondling her sensuous curves as I helped her clean up. By the time we finished with the rinse water I could tell that she was getting more comfortable with being naked in my presence. I took the opportunity to pull her to me for a kiss. Luckily, she didn't resist.

We had kissed several times before, but never while we were nude. I could feel her caution in her rigidness. I was getting a bit rigid, too, but only in one part of my body. When my growing erection pushed against her smooth flat belly, I could feel her pulling away. It took all the will power that I had to release from our embrace.

"Will you spend the night with me?" I asked politely. I didn't plead or beg. I couldn't let my arousal lead my conversations anymore. I needed to work my plan. If the plan included intimacy with a gorgeous woman, so be it.

"Sleeping?" she replied with a question of her own as she let her body dry in the stall. It was the best view I had received of her nude form so far since her arms were raised to avoid trapping moisture.

"Yes," I answered with a smile. "No sex until you are ready. I will hold to my promise."

I kept her close by sitting beside her at dinner. Strawberry walked in about halfway through our meal and gave me a questioning look. I responded with a nod of my own to let her know that I hadn't forgotten about her. But tonight, I needed to solidify my relationship with my number one girl.

After the meal I joined Cinnamon in her room in an attempt to make her feel more comfortable. She slipped under the covers with her panties on, but she did remove her bra. To my knowledge, she was the only member of the crew to wear one. But she certainly didn't need the support. Her breasts were as perfect as they had been in the shower. Small, round, and resting high all on their own. I did my best not to stare at them.

I got completely naked before joining her. My penis was chubbing up, but not quite erect. I saw her eyes linger on my package longer than I expected. Perhaps I had a chance at something more tonight, I thought. Then I reminded myself about my plan. Drawing Cinnamon close while keeping her comfortable with me was of the utmost importance. I could get myself off in private if my horniness became a problem.

"Are you getting an erection?" she asked with a shy grin as I slid up to her under the covers. The bite of her lip said that she liked it, but there was more than a touch of fear in her eyes.

"The boner can't be helped," I explained. "Just ignore it if you must. I will stick to my promise. You don't have to worry."

"You won't jab it into my belly again?" she asked playfully.

"No, I probably will," I answered. The only way I knew how to cuddle was with my front side against her. Maybe I should focus more of laying on my back and letting her drape over me as she saw fit.

She chuckled before replying, "There is no pleasure in rubbing it against my skin surely."

"Actually, there is," I told her. "Your skin is incredibly soft, though not lubricated like your special place. Combined with your beauty it is quite arousing."

Her smile disappeared. "You're not going to ejaculate on me, are you?"

"No, no," I responded while thinking, *yes, yes, oh hell yes, I would love to cum all over you.* "I'll be good. Trust me."

I made some small talk after that to get her comfortable. We chatted about the day, our work on the base and the repairs we had done. I asked her about her new best friend, Dawynda, the green dragon. She was blown away and even uncomfortable by all the attention that the female dragon was showing her. I told her to get used to it quickly. Having a powerful beast on her side could be quite an advantage in our future.

Despite the placid conversation my penis continued to be excited. I kept telling him that there wasn't going to be any sex tonight, but he had ideas of his own. Who could blame him? He was rubbing up against arguably the most attractive woman that I had ever shared a bed with. Of course, he was getting excited!

"Can I ask you a question?" I said after a pause in the conversation. We were facing each other and totally attentive to what the other was saying. Neither of us seemed very sleepy despite how active the day had been. When she nodded, I asked, "What is it like being a virgin these days?"

She made a face like she wished I hadn't addressed that particular subject. But she didn't refuse to answer. It just took her a moment to think about it.

"What do you mean?" she replied, looking elsewhere. I knew that was a sign that I needed not to push too much. "I guess biologically it is the same as your time."

"No," I smiled though she wasn't looking at me at that moment. "I mean society wise. In my time if you were sociable but a virgin, there would be a lot of pressure on you to have sex."

"Oh," she replied. "Well, nobody really knows but you."

"Honey and Coffee don't suspect anything?" I asked. I hadn't even considered the possibility that they others didn't know. "I mean, when you stop at space stations, don't you girls seek out male company?"

"Some do," she replied sheepishly. "I guess I did, too. But I never found anyone that I was comfortable with." There was a pause before she continued, "Until you."

"Oh!" I answered, getting more excited than I should. I reeled it back in before speaking again. "So, you anticipate me being your first?"

"Of course," she answered, barely glancing at my eyes as she spoke. "Just not tonight."

I stayed silent for a while until she returned her gaze to me. After a minute of searching each other's eyes, I asked, "Are you scared?"

Cinnamon took a deep breath and released it before nodding. "A little," she whispered.

"Do you know how sex works?" I asked.

I got attitude from her then. "Of course, I know how sex works!"

"Okay," I backpedaled a bit, trying to keep things lighthearted. Then a moment later. "How does it work?"

"Are you being serious?" she asked.

"Yeah," I responded. "I know that we will not be having sex tonight. I have accepted that fact even if my cock has not. But I thought we could still talk about it. I don't have a lot of experience..."

"Really?" she doubted me.

"But you have none. So, I thought you could share with me what you know. Then I can expand on that with my limited knowledge..."

"Limited, huh?"

"Then maybe you will feel a bit more comfortable when the times comes," I said. "I'm just thinking of you."

"Are you now?"

"Cinny. Surely you know how special you are to me. Nothing matters more than our relationship."

We stared at each other for a while after that. I firmly believed that I had said enough already. I deflected her attempts to draw attention to other lovers that I may have had and returned the focus to her. Either she was comfortable talking about sex or she wasn't. I would have to wait until she spoke again for the verdict.

"Well," she finally answered, looking everywhere around the room except for at me. "Your penis would go inside my vagina. You would have to be hard, of course. Kind of like you are right now. And I would have to be wet in order for you to slide in without you causing me pain. Though, considering the size of yours," she said as she briefly put her hand around it. "It's probably going to hurt anyway."

My breath caught in my chest when I felt her slender fingers around my rod. When she released, I asked her to continue, with her explanation, not with her hand.

"That's pretty much it," she said. "Isn't it?"

"That's the basics," I replied. "How would you achieve orgasm?"

"Oh," she answered bashfully. "Through the friction of the penetration mostly, I guess. I understand that inside of me there are some pressure points that help me climax."

"That's true. What else helps you along?"

"I don't know," she responded. I couldn't tell if she really had no other knowledge or if she was just playing shy.

"Do you put anything inside of you when you masturbate?" I asked, thinking it was a harmless question. Apparently, it was not.

Cinnamon had a shocked look on her face. I couldn't tell how much of it was real. "I'm not talking about that with you!"

I waited a moment to gauge the situation. Should I stop or press forward? Maybe she was just pretending to be horrified by the subject so I wouldn't think less of her.

"You don't have to say anything then," I eventually replied. "If you don't get off by penetrating yourself, I'm guessing that you mostly rub your pussy lips and your clit." She looked appalled at that statement, but I continued anyway. "You probably play with your breasts, too. Caressing the nipples if not pinching them."

The shocked look on her face only got worse. I was afraid to say anything more. There wasn't much else to say except for the more advanced stuff. And I wasn't about to suggest that she shoved anything up her butt or choked herself.

"How do you know this?" she asked, staring directly at me for once. Accusingly even. "Have you been spying on me?"

I laughed, but it obviously didn't make her feel any better. I had inadvertently tricked her into a confession. "No, Cinny," I told her with a gentle tone as I brushed her cheek with my fingertips. "I just have some idea of how the female body works."

"Oh," she said softly. It softened her expression, but not by much.

I waited for her to cool down before speaking again. Then I said coyly, "I'm going to fall asleep thinking about you touching yourself."

Smack! Right to my face before I could even see it coming. I blinked repeatedly in shock. Then I saw the smile on her face. She was just playing. Or maybe her instinctive reaction to my comment surprised even herself. I could see how curious she was to see my response.

"Okay, then," I decided to continue with the lesson. Perhaps I should draw attention away from her masturbation to make her more comfortable. "How do you get a guy to reach climax?"

"You mean you," she said. "You want to know how I would get you off."

"Yes, since I will be your first," I answered. "And hopefully your only..."

"Well..." she cut me off. I could tell that my timing was right. She was ready to talk more about sex. "Friction up and down your penis helps. I understand that the head is extra sensitive, so I should give it more attention. I could use my hands, or my mouth, or my vagina to get you to orgasm. And then there are the balls," she said. I felt her fingers caressing mine and I flinched at the unexpected touch. "They are delicate but can be used to accelerate things, I'm told."

I smiled at her and was happy to see her return it. Hearing her talking about sex was enough to get me hard as a rock. Her brief touches to my genitalia were getting my testicles working on manufacturing their product. I tried to tell all my private parts not to expect sex tonight, but they saw the signs and could not be convinced.

Then a curious look crossed her face. A moment later I felt the touch of a finger on the tip of my cock.

"Are you cumming?" she asked like a naïve little girl. "The head of your penis is wet."

"Oh," I replied, tempted to pull my groin back from her touch, but my cock wouldn't even consider it. "That is what they call precum."

"What is that?" she asked, resuming more of her student like demeanor.

"It... means… that I could cum soon, given the appropriate stimulus," I told her. "But don't worry about. I'm sorry if I got anything on you."

"My belly is a little sticky," she answered, not seeming all that annoyed by it. "I was just a little confused. I had not heard about precum. Does this mean that you are too far along that your balls will hurt if you stop now?"

"Ah," I answered. "You've heard about that." She nodded. "Well, I'll probably be okay. But honestly, it would be nice to get some release. Should I leave the room...?"

I was fishing for an invitation without making any movements to suggest that I was willing to go. A handjob, a blowjob, anything that she was willing to do. I could jerk it off myself if I had to. Especially if she'd let me cum all over those perfect little titties of hers.

"No," she replied as she began looking around for something. Then she grabbed a uniform shirt that she had discarded to the floor on a previous day. It wasn't the only piece of clothing just lying around. A neat freak she was not. "You can cum on this," she said. "I think I'd like to watch."

I raised an eyebrow as I shuffled out from under the blanket and onto my knees. My boner popped up like it was spring loaded once it cleared the covers.

"For a learning experience," she then said with big eyes focused strictly on my erection.

Stroking myself off in front of Cinnamon was not beyond what I was capable of. There was no doubt about that. But in a way, the act kind of made me feel used like the way Sage had done me.

"Are you sure?" I asked. "I could visit Coffee or Honeysuckle... or even Strawberry if you'd rather..."

"No!" she said, almost panicked. Then after a moment of regaining her composure she said, "I 'd rather that you stay. I know that I can't give you what those other girls can, but I'd really like for you to stay with me, if you don't mind. Just tell me what you need me to do."

Stroke it! Suck it! Put it between those titties! my boner screamed to my brain. Fortunately, I was too focused on my future to let him sway me. This time.

Did I want to have Cinnamon's hands and mouth on my cock and balls? Hell yeah! Who wouldn't? But I had to be careful to not have my sexual urges place a barrier between us. She was going to be especially important to my future. I kept telling myself that over and over again.

"Gently caress my balls," I told her as I started to stroke my shaft. I was delighted that she did not hesitate to oblige. We went like that for a minute or so before I made another request. "Take off your panties and lay in front of me with your legs spread," I said.

"You're not going to..."

"No," I assured her. "I just want to see your pussy while I stroke it, if that is okay."

She didn't move right away. I was beginning to think that I had asked too much. Eventually, though, she did as I instructed. With her bald, tan, cinnamon smelling pussy staring up at my cock I was in awe. The perfect skin. The symmetrical labia. That little dab of wetness at the entrance to her vagina. Her virgin pussy!

I stroked more feverishly as she watched. I was missing the touch of her fingers on my balls, but this was totally going to work.

"What else can I do?" she asked.

"Stroke it with me!" I answered immediately. I longed for the feel of her hands on me again.

"How?" she asked. Her unselfish personality was coming to the forefront. She genuinely wanted to help people in need. And I desperately needed her help in a bad way.

"I'll stroke the bottom half," I told her. "You stroke the top half with the mushroom tip and try to match my rhythm."

As soon as her hand touched my cock head, I knew it wouldn't be long. She focused on matching my strokes until it became too erratic. Then she just kept her tiny hand loosely round the tip as my pelvis thrusted, essentially fucking her hand. I grunted loudly as stream after stream of my sperm ejected from the hole to land on her belly.

Cinnamon was breathing heavily then. By the time that my ejaculation slowed to a dribble she was rubbing her pussy with a passion. She came just a few seconds after my brain came back online. I watched in amazement as she convulsed in front of me. It would have been just as awesome a few seconds earlier, but the realization that this was a big step forward for her was even more special.

Once Cinnamon stopped shaking, she pulled both hands to her face and started to cry. Her right hand had some of my semen on it, and her left hand was covered with her own sexual fluids. I was tempted to point that out until I realized how shaken she was. Her sobs got heavy as her tears poured out.

I ignored everything but the need to comfort my number one girl. She had just made a big sacrifice to hold on to my attention this evening. I had to show her some affection.

"What's wrong?" I asked.

She just shook her head. A moment later I asked again. She finally replied in a tiny squeak, "Nothing."

"It doesn't seem like nothing," I whispered to her. "Do you always cry after your orgasm?"

Cinnamon shook her head no.

"Are you sad?" I asked. I had made women cry before, but not like this.

"No," she mouthed the word without any sound as she shook her head again.

"Are you happy?" I asked then.

She nodded with a smile so full of tears that it looked like she was wincing in pain.

"Should I hold you?" I asked as I placed myself beside her on the bed, readying myself to accept her into my arms. She clung onto me like a scared child and continued to cry into my chest. It was not the most comfortable sexual experience that I ever had, but it was rewarding just the same.

Though we didn't have intercourse, we shared a super intimate moment, probably the most intimate moment of her life, and she followed it up with a desire to be in my embrace.

We drifted off the sleep like that, and I recalled Strawberry's recent words to me. She said that all I do is win, win, win. I was started to see things that way myself.

CHAPTER TWENTY-ONE:

Cinnamon was already gone when I woke up in her room the next morning. I found her in the galley with the rest of the crew eating breakfast. I was greeted in a friendly manner by everyone including Sage. There were more than a couple pairs of inquisitive eyes. I wasn't sure what Cinnamon had revealed about our night together. She had been such a private person regarding sexual matters that I doubted she said much. However, she had an afterglow that was lighting up the room.

Honeysuckle intuitively slid into the next seat to leave an empty space for me beside Cinnamon. I kissed my girl on the top of the head as I hugged her shoulders. She blushed something terrible as I slowly sat down next to her.

I had a very interesting thing going on. Relationships were building between me and nearly every woman on board the vessel. It was helping me rise through the ranks quickly. But I had only had vaginal sex with one of them so far. That felt peculiar.

I had been inside Coffee's hot pussy a couple times already. But I had only received handjobs from the others. In fact, all but Strawberry had played with my boner in the short time since I'd been with the crew. Of course, the experience with Sage was quite different from the others. Vanilla's situation was kind of weird, too. But all had brought me to orgasm except the leader.

I glanced at Strawberry wondering if she knew that she was only one left. She was smiling, but there was something fierce in her eyes. I certainly wasn't going to address it at the breakfast table, or in front of Cinnamon. I needed my best girl to enjoy this moment. She was clearly feeling special, even though what we had accomplished was essentially just mutual masturbation.

"Where's Teddy?" I asked, eager to change the subject before they start prying into my sexual life.

"In the cargo hold, of course," Sage replied. I expected her to say, *where he belongs*. But she didn't.

"I took him breakfast," Coffee announced from her spot on the other side of Cinnamon.

After a quick thought I decided this was an excellent opportunity for a power move. Everyone seemed to be in good spirits. With Strawberry making the stealthy move to my side this was a chance to gain more footing.

"I'd like for Teddy to have the freedom to move about the ship," I announced. "And to help outside."

Sage had a fork to her mouth about to take a bite. She stopped abruptly when she heard my statement. Then, realizing that all eyes were on her, she chewed her mouthful of synthetic eggs before speaking.

"I don't think that is a good idea," Sage said almost cautiously. Her typical overbearing tone was completely absent.

"He was a big help to me when I was doing repairs," Honeysuckle spoke up.

"I'm in charge of cargo," Cinnamon offered. "I can take responsibility for his welfare."

"His welfare is only part of the problem," Sage replied. "He is not part of this crew and never will be. Despite his apparent intelligence he must be treated like an outsider if not an animal."

"He shouldn't be allowed on the bridge," Strawberry finally spoke up. I studied her to see which way she was going to go on this issue. I knew she didn't want Sage to know that she would eventually be abandoning her, assuming that wasn't just a ploy. But she had disagreed with her leader before. "Or any sensitive areas of the ship without supervision. Other than that, I can take responsibility for his adherence to the rules inside. Kash? Do you think that he will listen to me?"

"Yes," I replied immediately, whether or not I thought that it was true. He had been taking instructions from Cinn and Honey. Would adding more females to his list push him over the edge? "I'll be with you when you address him the first time. I'll make sure that he understands."

It was a very brief conversation but an important one. Strawberry backed me instead of Sage, and I put myself in a position of authority on all things regarding Teddy. It wasn't a big promotion by any means, but a significant step just the same.

There was a period of silence as we continued our meal. I touched Cinnamon a few times to reconnect with her feelings after changing the subject. She responded timidly, but it looked like things were exceptionally good between us. I needed them to be.

"We are moving right along on repairs," Sage announced. "I read Honeysuckle's progress report this morning. From the looks of it we might be able to start engine and hull testing in a couple days."

All eyes went to Honeysuckle. This statement suggested that we were more than a week ahead of the original schedule. My idea of having crew members learn specific repair work had made an even bigger difference that I had imagined.

"Yes," Honey responded. "If we make good progress today and tomorrow morning, we might be able to fire up the engines for testing by tomorrow afternoon. We should be ready for hull testing the next day."

Everyone had a little more pep in their step as they went about their daily assignments and repair tasks. The thought of getting off this dreadful planet and back to their normal lives was a huge motivator for them. But was it for me? I wasn't sure.

Could I continue with my plan when all these women go back to a world that they know? I would likely be more lost on these space stations that I was when I first arrived here. And I would certainly be less valuable. Could I bring myself to ruin this opportunity for the women that I was starting to love?

Maybe I could just delay it for a bit. If I tried to mess with the ship I would surely be found out, though. That could set me back significantly in the eyes of my current followers. I didn't think it would be worth the risk. What could I do if anything?

Instead, I should work on putting myself in a better position. I was a quick learner and picked up on enough ship duty stuff to pass as a crew member, whether on this ship or another. But I didn't want to be just a crew member. I've got Teddy, but what would happen to him once we docked somewhere? Could I keep him safe?

I had Gako and Cinnamon had Dawynda. Two dragons were powerful allies. But not after we leave here. It is not like we would be taking them with us. Or could we?

The wheels were churning in my mind as I fixed the corner of one of the mist harvesters. A wofur had come right through our camp to head butt the contraption. It looked insane as it stumbled back to its feet and ran off, completely ignoring me standing just ten feet away with my sword drawn.

"Those clothes are not holding up very well," Strawberry said as she walked up behind me. I was squatting down and wondered if my hairy ass crack was showing. In this modern age body hair seemed to be much less popular according to the girls. But her comment was accurate. Their uniforms continued to look brand new as my lone set of shorts and button-down shirt were starting to become threadbare. At least all the blood stains had come out in the wash.

"As part of the crew," I said as I stood up. "I ought to be wearing a uniform."

The freckled red-haired hottie smirked at my terminology. I kept using words and phrases that had long been outdated. Just like my clothes.

"Maybe we can make one for you like we did Teddy," she laughed. It was really good to see her letting loose around me. "I'm honestly surprised that you don't just wear Koradd's or King's old uniforms. They should each have two sets in their closets."

"They do," I told her. "And King's fits reasonably well. I just didn't want to stir things up." His clothes bore a large C for captain.

"You are official now," Strawberry said. "I'm surprised that Sage hasn't ordered you to wear it."

"The clothes of the man that she presumably killed," I replied.

Her smile faded. Had I said something wrong or was she just sad about the loss of life? I waited for some kind of sign for what I should do next. Apologize? Confront her about Sage possibly being a murderer?

Strawberry didn't often lose control of her emotional state. The only other time that I had seen it was when she was about to go over the cliff. "Let's not talk about that," she finally said as her face returned to a pleasant disposition. "Let's talk about this meeting that you and I need to have."

"A meeting?" I asked.

"Yes," she grinned to let me know what kind of meeting she was talking about. "We have lots to discuss. Just the two of us. We can do it in my quarters. How about this evening after dinner?"

I nodded thinking that maybe she was just playing. But she wasn't, so I followed it with saying okay.

"Good," she said. "I look forward to it. I'm certain that we will both benefit from the exchange."

Then, as was her custom, she turned and walked away. Her hips swayed in exaggerated fashion. I couldn't take my eyes off her firm round ass. I fully expected her to turn and catch me, but she was too confident to do so. She knew very well that I was watching. Her effect on me did not need to be confirmed.

Later that day during a break I saw Gako lying on one of the thick flat branches in his tree. His head popped up when he saw me looking, so I decided to summon him to see how much influence I had on this powerful beast. I gestured with one hand in a come-hither motion.

Gako obeyed, or at least was intrigued enough to want to know why I beckoned him. He pushed with his strong rear legs to separate from the branch as he spread his wings to glide through the foliage. Though not crazy dense, there was not enough room to flap large dragon wings until he cleared the natural fortress shape of the tree. It was certainly a practiced and perfected method that made him look much more graceful than his resting fat lizard appearance.

Movement higher in the tree caught my attention. It turned out to be Dawynda, Gako's female. She was curious, too. I watched as she surveyed the area, perhaps looking for Cinnamon, before resting her head back on the branch.

"Have you ever thought about leaving this world?" I asked Gako.

He stared blankly at me for a moment before replying that he did not understand. Maybe he wondered if I was talking about the afterlife. Did dragons believe in such a thing?

"I'm talking about going to another world. A place vastly different from here. Some place where you will be unique. Respected and feared."

"I am respected and feared here," he answered. I shrugged and considered giving up the topic. It was a weird notion anyway to take Gako from his home world. Then he continued, "I cannot fly as high as you must think."

"You wouldn't have to," I told him with renewed interest. "You could go in our ship with us. It can fly off this world and through space to another planet."

Gako looked at the sky. "I do not understand space." I started to work on ways to explain it. His kind were not the type to ever develop interplanetary travel, so his confusion was understandable. "Would I be a prisoner like Teddy?" he then asked.

"No," I responded. "Not at all. And Teddy is no longer a prisoner either. You would be a passenger."

"Would the ship be my new home?" Gako was trying to comprehend the proposal. It was more than I expected. He usually kept his sentences very short when he lacked interest. "Or would another world be my new home?"

That was a good question. If I could somehow talk him into leaving with me, purely for selfish reasons of course, he would be trapped in the ship for long periods of time. The opportunities for him to spread his wings and fly would be few and far between. He would definitely feel like a prisoner much of the time. It wouldn't be long before he would want to stay on another planet or return home. I would lose all benefit from him joining me then. Would it be worth it to uproot him from his life here?

"A ball," Teddy's voice said from behind me. I was too deep in thought to realize that he was approaching, but Gako was watching my back. Nothing went without his notice.

I turned to see my little fuzzy orange friend with spherical gathering of leaves in his arms. He had woven a ball that was roughly one foot in diameter. I took it in my hands and stared in amazement. It was structurally sound enough for me to kick it. Teddy had quite a crafting skill that I had not been aware of previously. What else could he make?

"We play ball where I am from," he told me. "I understand that your people used to play ball back in your time on Earth."

"Yes," I replied excitedly. "We loved to play ball!"

I had been more into basketball than soccer, but a basketball court with hoops seemed to be too big of a project. I dropped the ball to the toe of my right foot and was pleasantly surprised in my ability to kick it back up to my hands. It was due more to the bounce in Teddy's design than my skill. The three of us stood there for a few minutes discussing ways that we could play sports with it.

By the time that Cinnamon approached I was dying to play some soccer. I had been out of my element for so long, struggling to learn how to live on this alien planet first, then on a spaceship with futuristic women. Just holding the ball gave me a warm feeling like I was home again.

I heard the flap of powerful wings as Cinnamon stopped at my side. Dawynda had taken notice and decided to join the party now that her favorite human had arrived. It took a few minutes to explain how to play soccer to the group. Teddy grasped it even faster than Cinnamon. The two dragons were mildly intrigued, but it was mostly because of my enthusiasm.

We found two large bushes about ten feet wide to serve as goals. The space between them was over two-hundred feet. That was more space than I needed, but Gako and Dawynda were several times my size. I took my dragon for a teammate and Dawynda naturally insisted on being on Cinnamon's team. She was more attached to my girl than to her own husband. Since I would surely be a better player than Cinny, I told Teddy to be on her team.

"That is an unwise decision," Teddy told me. His lip curled up to tell me that he was smiling. That is when I realized that he was talking trash to me.

"Oh, yeah? We'll see about that," I answered as I made exaggerated movements like a cocky ball player.

"You will regret this," Teddy replied in his typical monotone voice. He had the smack talking skill of a Harvard professor, but it was hilarious.

The ground between the two designated goals was reasonably flat, but certainly not smooth. There were also some smaller shrubs in the way. I had a few options of navigating the field while maintaining a soccer feel. I kept those in mind as I began my clumsy ball moving skills. Though never a great player as a child I expected to appear as a king of the sport in this environment.

My first move on Cinnamon was sloppy and the ball bounced off her shin. My second maneuver was much more impressive and sent the ball between her legs. Teddy was off to the left after that, so I moved right. Only Dawynda stood between me and the goal. She was standing there naturally, not in any style of athletic stance.

Gako was behind me and made no move to join my rush. No doubt he had no idea that he should. But that was okay. I was prepared to take it all the way myself and leave him on defense.

Teddy started that ape-like sprint that he does, using his long arms to propel his body forward substantial distances before his feet touched again. His momentum was considerable, so I decided to stop and pull the ball back as he flew by. Unfortunately, he had impressive stopping ability and punched the ball out from under my foot with his stubby little leg.

I turned to recover it at what must have seemed like a snail's pace compared to the Pithynos. Once he got control of the ball it never touched the ground again as he used his feet, head, and shoulders to keep it airborne just a few feet off the ground. I dashed after him but was too amazed by his skill to make a serious effort to catch him.

Gako took note of the athletic display and dropped into a stance that suggested he was about to pounce on Teddy. I hoped that there was no misunderstanding, and my little friend was in no actual danger. When Gako's tail swung toward the little guy I was overly concerned. But Teddy propelled himself high enough into the air to avoid being struck with what might have been deadly force. The ball rolled gently under the tail swing to rest close to the goal. Teddy landed nearby and kicked the ball into the bush before Gako could figure out what the fuck just happened. Despite being scored on, I laughed my ass off.

The rest of the game continued much like that with Teddy easily being the most valuable player. Both dragons eventually got the hang of things and contributed well both offensively and defensively. It quickly got much harder to score goals. Teddy toyed with me relentlessly, but I did happen to have a couple bright spots where I managed to steal the ball, even if it was only temporarily. The most impressive part of his play was how he managed to get Cinnamon involved. He would occasionally pass to her when it was totally unnecessary, just to have her contribute.

The score was seven to one before the game came to an abrupt halt. Teddy scored five times and assisted on Cinnamon goals for the other two. Dawynda could have scored herself, but she kept passing to Cinnamon instead, totally committed to the girl's success in the game. Our only goal was scored by Gako with a super high tail swing when his mate thought that he was going to go low instead.

It was when Gako halted suddenly in mid play that we all stopped what we were doing. He stared off into the sky at something approaching. It took me a few seconds to realize that it was a dragon. That was nothing new to see around here so I was confused. The only exceptional thing about the sight was how high the creature was in the air. At least a hundred feet, probably twice as high as I had ever seen a dragon.

"Get inside," Dawynda told us.

"What's wrong?" I asked.

"That's an orange dragon," Cinnamon answered. "We don't see them often, or by themselves."

"Yes," Dawynda replied as she put her wing around Cinnamon in a way to guide her toward the ship. "That is a scout. I don't know what he is looking for but if he sees humans here, he could draw more of them for an attack. He is almost close enough to smell you, too. Your perspiration has weakened your ability to block your scent. You must go back inside your ship now. Your little camp area will not be good enough."

"We'll stir up the dirt to mask your smell," Gako added.

"Won't just seeing the ship be enough?" I asked.

"I highly doubt that the thing knows what a spaceship is," Dawynda answered. "He'll just think it is a weird rock. The cargo cubes lined up will confuse him, but maybe not enough to draw a closer inspection. Go inside now, please. We don't want anything to escalate."

We followed the orange dragon's movements on the screen from inside the ship. There was no evidence to suggest that it was focused on us. It did circle around a few times nearby before flying over the canyon. I was impressed with its ability to stay airborne for so long. It had to be ten times longer than I had ever seen a dragon do before.

CHAPTER TWENTY-TWO:

After dinner I accepted Strawberry's invitation into her room. She kept her quarters tidy and free of clutter. There were three large photos on the wall opposite of her bed. The first was a close-up of herself holding a small computer tablet. On the screen was a notification that she had been hired as crew aboard the Arketa Koreta. The second was a photo of herself and an older man in a large hallway. He looked particularly sad. Behind them was a sign with bold letters saying CENTAURI. Above them in a cursive style font were the words Crimson Loop. Was that her father in the photo?

The third image was of a teenage girl smiling timidly. She had light brown hair and unremarkable gray eyes. A small girlish figure with none of the sass that Strawberry possessed. She was wearing some kind of uniform. I couldn't tell if it was for a job or a school. Due to her age, I got the feeling that it was the latter. The kind that I remembered from a private school on old Earth. Her face looked similar to Strawberry's. Could that be a sister? Surely it was not her daughter.

"I grew up on Crimson Loop Station Centauri," she said softly as she closed the door. She was not one to talk about her past much in our previous conversations. I was a little surprised that she would share anything personal with me. On the few occasions when our discussions weren't strictly business they were about sex. Not love, companionship or a relationship. Just sex.

"Is that your father?" I asked as I turned to face her. She looked so mellow compared to her normal self, like a facade came off once she entered the door to her private quarters.

"Yes," she answered like she was deep in thought, perhaps remembering her childhood. "His name is Stanson. We were close."

"Were?" I asked.

Strawberry shrugged and gave me that expression that said she was debating on saying anything more. I waited. Eventually, she told me that her father did not approve of her decisions as an adult, particularly her choice to leave the station. I knew there was a story there, but I didn't feel comfortable pushing any further. It was my intention to strengthen our alliance with this visit, not to create a barrier.

"And the girl?" I asked as I pointed to the third image. I was afraid to suggest that it might be her daughter, and that hesitation kept me from suggesting anything.

Strawberry's typical smile returned full force before she answered. "That's me, Kash."

"What?"

"I was fifteen then. I had not yet decided to go down the course that led to me leaving home.

"Oh," my mind caught up. "That was before your body modifications."

She nodded absently and she looked back at the picture of her younger self. "I keep it to remind me of who I was before I started this journey. It is very therapeutic."

I searched the photo for signs of Strawberry, the confident woman standing beside me. There wasn't much there. Judging solely by the photo I would have to assume that she had changed significantly since becoming an adult.

"Do you miss her?" I asked, trying to match the softness of her voice. This was a bonding moment for us.

Strawberry chuckled, the boldness of her personality returning to her stance. "Stars, no! I hated who I was. I keep that photo not as a memoir but as motivation to never be that weak again."

Oh shit! This was an even bigger story than I had expected. Would she reveal more? I was ready to curl up on the bed and listen to her talk about her childhood.

"We won't ever talk of it again," she then said flatly.

Well, there goes that idea. "Why do you let people in here if..."

"I don't," she cut me off. "You are the first to enter my quarters since I joined the crew. Except Sage. And she won't make that mistake again."

What the fuck! There was so much that I wanted to know. About her childhood and the factors that made her who she is today. About this incident with Sage. And about how much of that little teenage girl remained inside this confident woman. But I could clearly tell that she wasn't interested in revealing more. Not tonight anyway.

"So," she addressed me with a tone that clearly marked the beginning of a new conversation. "Should we talk first? Or fuck?"

Ummmm....

"There isn't much to say," she then said as she sat down on her bed. "So, let's talk first."

"There will be more fucking than talking?" I asked as I timidly took a seat at her feet.

"I sure hope so," she answered as she gestured for me to come closer. I was glad that I hadn't put my boots back on after my shower. They were really beginning to stink. I had been sure to not only clean up good for this meeting, but also to trimmed up my public hair. The shower stall had everything I needed for body grooming. Being my first time doing so in a while, I spent an extra fifteen minutes in there.

"So, what is it that you want?" she asked. At first, I thought she meant sexually. Should I ask for a blowjob? A titjob, too? I was still trying to figure out what was appropriate when she spoke again. "I mean, you obviously want power. But how high are you expecting to go? And what are you planning to do once we leave this planet?"

Oh! Good thing I didn't speak quickly.

"I'm not sure," the words slipped out of my mouth. I hadn't really wanted to admit that. But since I did, I figured maybe I should get more real with her. Perhaps she would trust me more. "I just don't want to be oppressed."

"Oppressed?" she laughed.

"Bossed around, taken advantage of, that kind of thing."

"You mean like having your cock stroked to the point of ejaculation, then refused that satisfaction?" she asked. She smiled at my shocked look. "Yes, she told me about that. So, I completely understand where you are coming from. I just want to know how far you are prepared to go."

I didn't have an answer for that question. At least not one I was prepared to speak out loud. However, since she was addressing the matter, she surely had some ideas of her own.

"What is it that you suggest?" I asked, cutting to the chase.

"Well," she replied, noticeably hesitant about revealing her plan before hearing mine. "I think we can run this ship together. Sage can fall in line or be dropped off at the next station."

"Or planet," I muttered.

"I wouldn't do her like that," my new berry friend said. "She's not entirely bad, but she does have some serious issues. The other girls will happily follow you. Vanilla will follow me. I have the knowledge that we need to survive in this galaxy. We will never have to report back to King's company again. All profit from our excursions will be ours to split. How does that sound?"

"Good," I admitted. Better than I expected even. Of course, that gave me some concern. When things were being presented to look too good to be true, they usually were. "So, would we be a couple then?"

"Oh, stars fucking no!" she laughed. "Don't get me wrong. I'd love to have you as a fuck toy. But our relationship would otherwise remain professional. Considering your interest in Cinnamon, Honeysuckle and Coffee, it is probably best for you as well. Agreed?"

"Sure," I replied. I could certainly work with that. I definitely preferred not to burn any bridges in building my alliance with Strawberry.

"Excellent!" she said as she stood up off the bed. "It is all settled then. We'll follow each other's leads as we get this all worked out, just like we have been doing."

I stood up confused. Was the meeting over? Was I being asked to leave now?

Strawberry saw the bewildered expression and clarified matters. "You aren't going anywhere yet," she explained. "I'm just taking my pants off."

I watched as she pulled the uniform shorts down to her ankles to kick them off. She had a neatly trimmed fiery red bush. I was surprised that there weren't any freckles around her hips or ass. Simply perfect porcelain skin. She had no panties on. I rushed to remove my own shorts and boxers along with them.

"You may only touch my hips," she then told me. "At least this time. We may graduate to more intimate positions in the future. For now, just sit on the edge of the bed with your legs spread."

I did as I was told and watched in awe as she backed up that sexy ass of hers to my groin. Her skin was unbelievably clean and white right up until her pussy. Her lips there were bright red like a prostitute's lip stick. I wasn't quite hard yet, but I was getting there the longer I looked at her backside. She had the Marilyn Monroe of rear views.

She reached back between her legs and grabbed my penis. After a couple brief strokes to test its firmness she began rubbing it against her pussy lips. A few seconds later I could feel her moisture on my tip. She used my cock head to rub the wetness all around the hole, getting her whole crotch well lubricated.

Neither of us spoke as she took responsibility for our preparedness. She stroked me a few more times to make sure that I was stiff enough for her mount. Then she slid down on top of me.

She moaned and stopped after just a couple inches. Letting out a breath she rose up slightly to give it another try. This time she went halfway down my shaft and let out a deep groan. I stayed quiet, but I was feeling the same way. I continued to watch as those unbelievably red pussy lips swallowed my flesh sword inch by inch. Her vagina was tight and unusually hot. The sensitive skin of my penis almost felt like it was burning.

Once the penetration was complete and accepted, she began bouncing up and down on me. Slowly at first, but her rhythm continued to increase until it matched that of a stripper's lap dance during a heavy metal song. It certainly wasn't what I was expecting when I entered her room, but it was still incredibly enjoyable. More for my cock than for my ego, though.

I finally remembered that I was allowed to touch her hips. I let my hands rest there as she went about the business of high-speed thrusting on my shocked boner. She certainly did not need my help with her method.

"Oh, Kash!" she moaned. "Oh, Kash, I'm cumming on your big cock!"

She got even hotter and wetter inside there. Then it started splashing out onto my belly and balls as she plowed herself with my rigid ramrod. I started grunting with each bounce. Between the sight of it, the feel of it, and her thorough enjoyment, I was about to get off myself.

"Fuck it!" she yelled as she grabbed my hands and encouraged me to finally participate. "Fuck my hole!" she screamed.

I thrust upward awkwardly at first, but soon was able to match her rhythm. It felt even better to have some control. I was reaching climax in a hurry.

"Fuck it, Kash!" she screamed again. It was loud enough to make me wonder how soundproof these walls and doors really were. Then she grabbed my balls firmly. "Give me all of your cum! I demand it!"

My orgasm was so strong that it hurt at first. Or maybe that was her grip on my testicles. I released my seed into her fiery vagina almost happy that it was over. I had never been fucked quite like that before.

Her fingers became relaxed as she massaged my balls, whispering, "Give it all to me. Don't make me force it out of you."

I didn't know what that meant but I didn't like the sound of it.

"That's all of it!" the words burst from my mouth. "There isn't any more!"

Strawberry laughed hysterically for a few seconds then finally dismounted. She then reached into a drawer and grabbed what looked like a narrow red dildo. It was only about half as thick as my cock but maybe six inches long. Then unceremoniously she shoved it up her woo. What was that about? I was afraid to ask. I watched in confusion as she pulled her uniform shorts back over that sweet ass.

Strawberry picked up my boxers and shorts from the floor and slid them on for me. I stood up wondering what to do next other than fasten my pants. Before I could finish, she pulled my body against hers. A soft sensual kiss that lasted only a few seconds was followed by a second one. Then she opened the door for me to leave without saying another word. Her wide grin and afterglow told me that she was satisfied with the meeting.

Without a doubt, so was I.

CHAPTER TWENTY-THREE:

Excitement was buzzing in the air. All absolutely essential repairs had been completed on the spaceship. Strawberry ran a system analysis to return a seventy two percent chance that the engines would pass their test. The hull was given just a forty-four percent chance, but I was told the computer was programmed with unrealistic parameters for a safe hull. That didn't sound right to me, but nobody else spoke up against it, so I stayed quiet. I would think that a passing grade on the barrier that would protect us from the cold void of space would be a high priority.

I had never been higher off a planet than what an airplane could take me. And that was alarming at times. Our busted up and patched together craft had to take us much higher. So far that we would leave the planet's atmosphere. There would no longer be ground below us and sky above. That was as scary as shit to me. Add to it the fact that this particular spaceship had a history of crashing (just once but still), and I could feel myself beginning to get sick as I thought about launching.

I did my best to hide it, but I was certain that I was being too quiet. However, when I tried to be more talkative it came out like it was forced. I needed to come to terms with it and move on. Put it out of my mind. It wasn't like I would consider staying behind as the lone human on a dragon infested planet with no structure for safety.

I talked to both Gako and Dawynda about what it would be like to get on the ship and soar through space from one planet to the next. Or from station to station. If I had my say we would be spending a lot of time on the surface of planets. In my mind they should be overly concerned about their lives and future to do such a thing. I think that I wanted them to be more scared than me to make me feel better. But the plan backfired.

They both said that they were interested in going with us.

Could anyone imagine that? Full grown dragons on a human spaceship. Wandering around on a human space station. Passing customs and security at each stop. Getting a room at a hotel. Nope.

I joked about it with Strawberry as a way to continue our bonding. Her reaction was almost as surprising as Gako's willingness to go.

Strawberry thought that it would be a great idea. On top of that, she was certain that Sage would agree.

Cargo. Animals to be sold at the next stop. That's what Sage would have in mind. Possibly Strawberry, too. Maybe that had already been part of their plan. I couldn't be sure. With the backing of my other friends, including Teddy, I believed that we could keep them free. But to what end?

Dragons would never be able to live like humans. Even if they were willing to go, why would I do that to them?

Before the engine testing, I decided to show Gako and his wife the cargo hold where they would have to spend much of their future time if they chose to go with us. I totally expected it to be a deal breaker. Instead, they walked right in and got cozy. Then the list started. Things that they wanted to take with them. A piece of the red tree. Foliage for snacking on. Some packed meat from the animals that made up most of their diet. Also, Teddy's woven leaf ball was on the list.

I had a vision of the ship getting knocked off course because of two dragons slamming into a side wall while playing soccer. It was hilarious, but preposterous.

"Engine testing begins in five minutes," Sage's voice came across the speaker.

I hurried our mega-lizard friends out of the hold and to a safe distance while they were still wondering where the voice had come from. The tests weren't supposed to cause damage to our surrounding area, including our makeshift camp, but I didn't want to take any chances.

Everyone was on the bridge except Vanilla and Honeysuckle when I arrived. I had to be there to monitor the screens at the pilot's station. They said that it was valuable experience before we actually take flight. I had completed thirty-seven hours of flight simulator in addition to the training courses, so I didn't see the big deal, but there was nowhere else to be anyway.

Honeysuckle stayed in the engine room. I had a bad feeling that she would get hurt again so I asked Teddy to stay with her. At first, he gave me a look like I was putting him in harm's way. When Honey told him how much it would mean to her, he relented. I could clearly see that he was finally warming up to the girls of the crew.

Forty-two minutes passed by as the ship repeatedly rumbled then calmed, followed by a long list of status reports. The few items that came back red as failures ended up being corrected by programming adjustments. No additional repairs were needed. The ship's computer declared the engines flight ready.

"I need you to move your things back to the pilot's quarters," Sage told me as we were leaving the bridge. Perhaps she expected a fight over it. But it made sense to me. Koradd's old room had been repaired. My job was pilot. And that put me back on the same side of the ship as Cinnamon. I considered asking if Sage was going to take my place in the captain's quarters but decided against it. If this was her attempt to pick a fight, I wasn't going to give her the satisfaction.

"Sounds good," I replied and walked away without waiting for her reaction.

I ran back outside to find both green dragons waiting for my return. I had no more repairs to do. My pilot training was complete. All that was left was to start moving everything back inside. Our outdoor camp was much more short-lived than I had expected. But it did provide some benefits for several days.

"We have talked about your proposal," Dawynda said as I approached. I thought, finally, they've come to their senses. Dragons in space? Ridiculous!

"I will need Cinnamon's word that we will be safe," the large female dragon told me. "In addition to the list of essentials that we provided."

"Excuse me?"

"She must vouch for our safety among the cargo in your ship during flight," Dawynda continued. "As well as any place where we would disembark."

"Are you serious about this?" I asked.

"And she must vow to return us home if at any point we are unhappy with the arrangement."

That was a tall order, I thought. I was sure that Sage or Strawberry would guarantee them anything to get them onboard. But Cinnamon? I had yet to catch her in a lie. To my knowledge she was as honest as they get these days. She would be more than hesitant to guarantee their safety. And that would break the deal and make them stay put for their own good. The only thing that bothered me was that they wouldn't take my word for it.

"Why Cinnamon?" I asked. "Don't you trust me?"

"Mostly," Gako replied. He was always brief in conversation, which worked well considering how slowly he spoke. His woman on the other hand...

"No, Kash," Dawynda said plainly. "You have a struggle inside of you. I can sense it. You have done bad in the past and that tendency is still with you. I believe that you mean us well, but that could change should a great opportunity arise. I will not take that risk. Cinnamon, however, is the purest heart among you. What she vows she will do."

"She might not have control over every situation," I told them. There was no reason to debate her reason for trusting Cinnamon over me. I would do the same. "Despite good intentions, even she could let you down."

"If she vows," Dawynda dipped her nose toward my face almost in a threatening manner. I got the impression that she was offended by what I said. "She will do. Cinnamon will find a way to uphold her promises. I believe that wholeheartedly."

"Well, she'll be out soon. You can ask her yourself. But for the record, I wouldn't promise you those things. And I can be trusted by my friends. Any deception or treachery you sense in me is reserved for my enemies."

Dawynda got even closer. Her hot steamy breath caused me to blink my eyes, but I held my ground. "How many times," she asked slowly, "have your friends become your enemies?"

I couldn't help but think back to my past. *Fuck you!* I thought in my mind. How could she possibly know me this well? Had she been talking to Teddy? I hadn't revealed much about my past to the little guy, but he was incredibly intuitive himself.

"Also," Dawynda told me. "You forgot to put on your mud. You smell like a sweaty human steak." Then she licked her lips and smiled.

It was not the first time that I had exited the camp area without the scent blocker. The mostly confined camp had provided us with a measure of protection that we were getting out of the habit of pasting up before going outdoors. My own orders, though, were that no one exits the base without that protective cover.

I returned to safety and started tagging the cargo containers by number. Cinnamon already had worked out where each one would go back inside the ship. She was going to program the loader to move them as needed. We were cautioned to stay out of its way as it did so. It would be much faster than her controlling the huge robot manually but had some inherent risk. Its ability to sense the proximity of fleshy lifeforms and avoid injuring them was limited.

Then I began disengaging the roof canopy from the cubes. As the loader went about its business, I could be working on the more difficult task of removing the attachments from the top of the hull. But the rest of the work would have to wait until the next day. It was already past dinner time. I would likely be eating by myself.

That turned out not to be the case, though, as both Coffee and Cinnamon waited in the galley for me after completing their meals. They were sitting across from each other which made me choose which one to sit by. Considering her importance in upcoming matters, I chose Cinnamon. Coffee obviously looked disappointed.

I had chosen strategy over sex. My loins regretted it when Coffee left us a couple minutes later, but I was mostly proud of myself.

I told Cinnamon about Gako's and Dawynda's demand that she guaranteed their safety from the moment that they step onto our ship, and vow to return them should they be unhappy.

"I can't guarantee that," she said with a concerned look.

"I know. It's probably best that they don't leave their home anyway."

"Will you not miss them?" Cinny asked me as she slid her hand into mine. I didn't need it to eat so I gladly accepted the affectionate gesture.

"I will," I admitted. "But I'd rather miss them than watch them die or be sold."

"That is a good point," she replied. "But I can't help feeling like we need to take them with us."

"Really?"

"Yes," she nodded. "And Teddy feels the same way."

Teddy? Why would he want them to go? For his protection? Or maybe he thought they would take the attention away from him and be sold first. Surely two dragons would be worth more than a Pithynos.

Cinnamon saw the confusion on my face. "He thinks that you will need them for protection. I told him how you are an outsider and will not likely be treated the same way at our space stations as you have been by the crew."

"I see."

"I'm going to make the vow to Dawynda," Cinnamon surprised me. "But I need you to help me keep that vow. Can you do that?"

"I can try," I answered still bewildered. "But I can't guarantee anything."

"You have bonded with Strawberry, have you not?"

"Bonded?" I asked, unsure of what she meant. I studied her face for a clue.

"The two of you have had sex, I know," she told me with a bashful bow of her head. "I'm sure that has helped you two form an alliance. I believe with her help we can protect all our friends."

We talked some more after I showered. She helped me move my limited personal items from the captain's quarters to the pilot's bedroom. I decided to take the dead guy's uniforms with me. It would be best to fit in when we make contact with other humans after leaving this planet. I would have to look into having the C removed from the top. Or not.

Cinnamon was happy to spend the night with me, but we never got past cuddling. I caressed her here and there to try to get her aroused, but she just snuggled against my chest. She even swatted my hand away a couple times. I couldn't help thinking if maybe I had just sat on the other side of the table I could have been balls deep into Coffee's sweet pussy by then. But that would simply get me another orgasm. In the days ahead there were certainly going to be more important things than sex. And Cinnamon was going to be a key player, I believed.

After breakfast I went outside to prep for the cargo cubes getting reloaded. A bunch of stuff from the roof assembly was lying in the way. I needed to clear a wide path for the loader before I started on detaching things from the hull. I was several minutes into my work when I saw Dawynda looking at me curiously from her perch in the tree. That's when I remembered that I forgot to put on the skin covering mud.

Cinnamon and I both got dirtied up together. She joined me when I returned outside to check the area for any problems that might interfere with her loader program. Once she was certain she set the thing in motion. I climbed the ladder to start removing hooks and cables from sections of the roof of the ship. I was halfway through when I heard Coffee calling for me.

I crawled over to the edge to find her on the lower rungs of the closest ladder. She was not one to wander outside without reason. Whatever she had to say must be important. I noticed the concerned look on her face but wasn't sure if it was because of any news that she had to share or her discomfort with being out of the safety of the ship.

That's when I noticed that she had no mud on her skin. I could clearly see the pulse of her special intricate tattoo. She came out to find me in a hurry, not realizing how far from safety I would be.

I heard a flap of wings and looked directly to the red tree where the two friendly dragons were calling home lately. Dawynda had just cleared the branches but Gako was right behind her. However, it was not their wings that I heard.

An orange dragon was heading straight for us, flying just a few feet off the ground. Not as large as our greens, but they were known for being fierce. And it was much closer than our friends.

"Climb up here!" I yelled to Coffee, intent on protecting her. My sword was already in my hand with the blade exposed.

She had turned to see the approaching threat and did the opposite of what I told her. It made sense not to climb up when a killer dragon was coming at you, but there was no one to protect her on the ground. There was some scattered debris and a few cargo cubes, but they were too far away to reach in time.

Cinnamon had the pistol, and she was currently inside. I only had the sword. Teddy carried the shocker pistol when he went outside, but last I checked he was helping Honeysuckle with preparations for the hull tests. Coffee herself was weaponless.

"Get down!" I yelled at her, but she was too scared. She ran as fast as she could for the tail end of the ship. Before she could turn the corner, the orange dragon was on her.

Knife like talons dug into her flesh through her uniform as she screamed. I retracted my blade and jumped from the top of the hull. The ground was over twenty feet below me. It was stupid but I was desperate to save Coffee. I was fortunate that the sloped canopy supported my weight where it was still attached and formed a steep slide.

I made it to the ground safely but rolled twice before coming to a stop. I looked up just in time to see the orange dragon flying away with Coffee kicking and screaming in its clutches. Then it went out of view past the tail end of the ship toward the cliff.

Dawynda passed by at full speed an instant later in pursuit. Gako stopped to take a defensive stance on top of one of the cargo units, turning away from me. He spotted more threats.

I got to my feet to see the most curious sight on a slight hill not far away. Two men approaching, dressed like I had been in khaki shorts and shirts. Theirs were in even worse shape than mine.

The portal.

They must have come through the portal before me. I knew that there were others. I just hadn't considered the possibility that they had survived. If it weren't for Coffee's life being on the line, I would have a list of questions for them. But there was yet another discouragement involved.

They had more orange dragons with them.

CHAPTER TWENTY-FOUR

I wanted to run to the cliff and find out what happened to Coffee. Did Dawynda manage to save her? But I can't. I have to deal with the current and more significant threat.

I tried to focus as I slowly stood and took a few steps toward our new enemy. I was still wearing my portal duds just like them. I drew attention to my clothes, but the other two guys just laughed. Perhaps they had gone insane during the time that they had spent on this planet. If I hadn't met these six magnificent women, maybe I would have as well.

The man on the left was downright fat with a long beard draped onto his protruding belly. He looked taller than me, too, but certainly shorter than his companion. The other man might have been seven feet tall, and broad chested. His skull looked a bit overgrown like a dim-witted giant from the movies. They both looked like criminals for sure. Did I come across like that when Cinnamon first saw me? No wonder she acted the way that she did.

Gako let out a roar that was matched by all five of the opposing dragons. I took it as a declaration that neither party were prepared to stand down. The orange variety of the winged beasts appeared to be just slightly smaller than the green, but noticeably less bulky. Wiry like Velociraptors, I figured.

I had gotten used to the smell of burnt antifreeze associated with Gako and Dawynda's presence. It was strong enough to block out other scents, though. But not this time. An overwhelming barrage of dirty gym sock stench bombarded my nostrils. I knew that it had to be the signature odor of the orange dragons. There was no way the two men could smell that bad. However, they obviously made no attempt to mask their body odor. Perhaps traveling with five fierce flying lizards eliminated the need for such a precaution.

Six flying lizards, actually. One of them had taken Coffee a moment ago. It returned with a thud of its dead weight on the ground, neck nearly snapped in two. Dawynda had dropped it just on the other side of the few remaining cubes for dramatic effect. Then she joined her husband on top in a protective stance. There was no sign of my dark-skinned lover.

The addition of the second opposing beast and the loss of one of their own did not appear to have much effect on our attackers. They did have us outnumbered five to two in the reptilian department. And two to one on human fighters. Though I was incredibly happy with the effectiveness of my sword, it probably didn't wow them from more than fifty feet away. I was glad to see that all the two men had for weapons were the machetes that we brought from Earth.

The loader returned for another cargo cube but stopped short of lifting it. Its head rotated slowly as all in attendance watched. Then it reached onto its back to swap its arm attachments for something that could grip a smaller object. After installed it reached into its lower frame to grab two electrified cutters that Cinnamon had attached after our last battle. She must have ended its program and took over manual control. I just hoped that she was able to be effective from inside the ship. Surely, she would not be coming outside into this mess.

My concern for Coffee was distracting, but I couldn't put it completely out of my mind to focus on the task at hand. Had she been killed? Was she clinging to the side of the cliff, waiting for me to rescue her? Or lying wounded just on the other side of the ship?

Both of the crew's firearms were inside our spacecraft. Cinnamon had the pistol. The rifle would be resting in the locker until it was needed. Last battle Strawberry came out to support. Late, but better than not at all. Would she do so again?

"Go!" one of the men yelled. The fat scraggly one. And all hell broke loose!

Five mean orange dragons raced forward just a few feet off the ground not bothering to hide their intent. Two went straight for Gako, two for Dawynda, and one for me. They did not care about the loader.

Gako flew forward toward his attacking pair, deked one way, then flew the other to impact with one of the two dragons. He managed to pin the thing down and get a good bite on the thing's neck before its partner arrived. Then he had to let go to protect himself. The momentum of the second attacker sent Gako into a roll, but it looked like he was able to keep from getting bit.

Dawynda waited for her two patiently. They arrived at the same time which seemed at first to be a bad plan. But a vicious tail swing sent one of them out of play for a few seconds so she could focus on the other. She seemed to be able to dominate the smaller dragon easily, biting a forward leg clean off. Before the other attacker returned, I had my own battle to worry about and lost view of my friends.

The evil looking, howling orange dragon came at me like a corkscrew. Maybe its body was flying straight, but the head kept swirling. Perhaps it was a tactic to protect its neck. I stepped forward at the last second with my shiny blade forward. It was enough to get the thing to pull up slightly. I took advantage of the adjustment and dropped to the ground on my back as it flew overhead, its head too far to snap at me. My blade pressed upward sent a deep cut into its less protected belly from shoulder to groin. The beast screamed as dark blood erupted from the wound splattering all over me.

I rolled up onto my knees to wipe the dark liquid from my face, my mind scrambling with how to survive the next pass. If these things were as smart as the black dragons it would not fall for the same trick. It was the largest reptile I had faced except for the blues that nearly killed me when I was recording the hull damage. Back when Gako had come to my rescue. But he was much too busy to help me now.

All four feet touched down as the jumbo lizard rotated back toward me glancing at its belly wound briefly. A roar that sounded more like a cry bellowed from its jaw just before it came at me. I braced myself still trying to figure out what to do. Both its neck and its tail were longer than my sword.

A flash of shiny metal came from my left to collide with the animal. The loader. One of the blue cutters struck the dragon's eye and went straight through the head. It struggled against the machine and was on the verge of tipping it over despite what I had thought would be a mortal wound. I recovered from the shock quickly and jabbed my sword into its chest where I figured the heart might be. The squirming slowed as it fell onto the ground.

I turned to face the rest of the battle in time to see both men approaching. One was headed for me and the other for Gako.

Dawynda appeared to have killed one of her foes already and was wrestling with the other, each trying to get their jaws around the other's neck. Gako still had two attackers on him, but one looked to be wounded enough to almost even things up. He would be vulnerable to the man joining in. I had to help.

But once again, I had my own attacker to worry about.

The tall one was coming at me cautiously. As I waited the loader whirred by me with its blue light cutters swinging. The man dipped under one side to avoid getting cut and stepped right into my reach. Without hesitation I swung my sword in a circle above my head, samurai move style. The sharp blade went straight threw the man's neck at an angle, taking part of his shoulder with it. The shocked look on his face as his head rolled onto the ground was alarming. I had never seen anything like that in real life before.

I then heard the sound of the energy pulse rifle. It left a series of scorched marks on the ground at the feet of the heavy-set bearded guy. He had been staying back so Strawberry had a clear shot at him. It was too dangerous to try and snipe one of the enemy dragons as they were tangled with our friendlies. I hoped my new berry girl realized that and wouldn't sacrifice one of our own to win the battle.

Mister Beardo retreated behind some tall bushes as the battle raged on. Dawynda looked to be getting tired. She had maintained an advantage, but her stamina was less than the ferocious orange fuckers. The weakest one that I previously thought was dead, was chewing at one of her rear ankles as the other was flapping its damaged wings wildly to get onto her back. She decided to beat the one on the ground with her massive tail, but the angle was poor and didn't do as much damage as expected. The thing refused to release. Her neck twisted this way and that as her jaw snapped at the airborne attacker.

Gako was in even worse shape. One of the beasts had his head pinned to the ground as the other bit and scratched at his belly. I began sprinting to his aid with my sword forward when I saw something scurrying across the ground toward me. Teddy was let outside when Strawberry opened the door and appeared to be eager to help his new friends.

The fuzzy orange monkey like creature swung quickly up to the top of the loader to take one of the cutters. He then swung himself onto the dragon that had Gako pinned down. A rapid succession of stabs into the dragon's eye sent him convulsing to the ground. Gako quickly recovered and bit the other one right on top of the head. It totally didn't expect it.

I arrived shortly after that and cut the thing's lower tail off. When it turned its attention to me Gako went for the kill and snapped the beast's neck.

Dawynda rolled forward onto the ground to do a flip. It placed the ankle biter on top of her, but that maneuver separated them from the one that was trying to land on her back. The new configuration gave Strawberry a clean shot. Three holes appeared in the flying orange dragon's body. One in the wing, the other two in its back. It dropped to the ground and tried to run off, but it was in too bad of shape.

The loader rolled over to Dawynda's position and distracted the last remaining attacker enough that she could get a good grip on it. At first it looked like she was trying to put him into a headlock. I wasn't sure that her arms, which were more like front legs were long enough to do so. Then her tail flew up to wrap around its neck. In some kind of wicked dragon martial arts maneuver she snapped the creature's neck in a way that its head hung to the side like it was almost detached. When she let go of it the body dropped into the tall grass motionless.

Both dragons were injured and bleeding, but they had no trouble standing. Neither I nor Teddy sustained any wounds. Strawberry managed to keep to a safe enough distance that no attacker even came close to her. The men did not have any guns and that made a big difference in how things played out.

The bearded guy did not reappear. All of his dragons died in the battle. Or at least all that he had with him. If he was able to bond with them or train them somehow, he could likely do it again and return with a larger force. It would be a good idea to be gone before he did.

I ran to the other side of the ship in hopes of finding Coffee, maybe unconscious but still alive. She wasn't there. I looked over the edge of the cliff thinking maybe she was clinging to or climbing up the side.

From my vantage point I saw nothing but birds. The ground beyond the drop off was too far away. More than a hundred feet down.

I quickly went back to Dawynda. "What happened to Coffee?" I asked.

"She dropped," the green dragon responded. I could hear fatigue in her voice. Maybe grief as well.

"From where?" I asked, my voice cracking.

"I'm sorry, Kash," Dawynda said, making the effort to look me in the eye. "I was too late to save her. She hit the ground below about the same time that I reached her killer."

"You saw her hit?" I asked, unable to choke back the tears. Strawberry stood there in shock at what she was hearing. She had no idea that Coffee had even been outside let alone taken away. That also suggested that she did not know what the young woman was racing to tell me.

"She could not have survived," Dawynda answered before turning away. Her head seemed heavy. She slowly laid down on the ground to rest.

"They are both badly injured," Teddy said to me solemnly. "Is there something that Doctor Vanilla can do for them?"

"What?" I responded, unable to focus on anything but the loss of my coffee flavored friend. My lover. And the most carefree happy of my followers. With her went a big piece of my heart, and possibly my mind for the time being.

"Probably," Strawberry answered. She had been distraught at the news of losing a crew member, but her relationship with Coffee was quite different than mine. She then used her communicator to tell Vanilla that we would be bringing two injured dragons into the cargo hold to rest and heal. Anything that she could do to help would be appreciated.

There wasn't a scratch on me, but I felt so drained emotionally like I was near death. When Cinnamon came out to see the aftermath, she had the pistol with her. When I gave her the news about Coffee, she released the pistol, dropped to her knees and placed her face in her hands. Heavy sobs followed as I joined her down there and wrapped my arms around her.

CHAPTER TWENTY-FIVE

Strawberry tried to lead Dawynda and Gako around to the back of the ship. They would need to then go between the two large engine sections to reach the entrance. Though the dragons were huge compared to us, they would easily fit through every door on the ship due to their shape and agility. They only needed to make it into the cargo hold, though.

Dawynda refused to follow the redhead and Gako was content to follow his wife's decisions on the matter. Their weakened condition might be making them less agreeable. I tried to snap out of my stupor and tell them that it would be okay. In my current state, though, I was anything but convincing. It wasn't until Cinnamon wiped away her tears that we got them to move in the right direction.

"Please," Cinnamon told her devoted dragon. "Come into the ship. For your protection while you heal. I think our doctor can help you get back to full strength quickly. You don't have to stay. Before we launch Kash and I will make sure that you have the opportunity to exit the ship. I promise."

Without hesitation Dawynda followed her girl around the engines and through the entrance. Gako was right behind her, both of them limping and dragging tails that would normally swing gallantly. I'm glad they went inside. Lacking energy to fight they could be easy prey for this world's predators.

I had come to think of myself as the dragon whisperer until recently. It had become apparent that my influence over Gako paled in comparison to Cinnamon's on Dawynda. With Gako so trusting of his female companion, my girl actually controlled both of them. That made her even more than me in that regard.

Though it would not be easy to get over losing Coffee, I knew I needed to focus on other things at the moment. These were important days. Hours even.

Coffee was such a lovable free-spirited young lady. Absolutely beautiful with her brown skin and short curly blonde hair. A seductive lean body that was very enjoyable to play with. And passion, my goodness. Our sexual encounters were wonderful. I was missing her badly already. But I couldn't feel sorry for myself. I had other women. But Coffee's life was over. And it had to be at least partly my fault.

She had come out of the ship in a hurry to tell me something. She hadn't bothered to block her scent. I assumed that was in haste, but we had gotten used to moving around inside the camp without the fake mud. Coffee, however, was never a big fan of spending time outside. She usually only went when I asked her to join me.

What was she going to tell me?

I thought back to Strawberry as she walked by my side behind the dragons to enter the asshole of the ship. The only entry point that I knew of except an emergency hatch on top that would require some effort to open and close. The double lock system of the hatch was not automated, and it required climbing a ladder embedded into the wall at the top of the steps to reach it. But what I was really thinking about was what the redhead had said to me. She wanted to be at my side as I took control of the ship. More like a partner than a follower. But she did say that she would only share that position with Cinnamon.

With Cinnamon's dragon control and Strawberry coming to my aid twice, that idea was looking good. However, that left out Honeysuckle. Sure, I was crass enough to push her aside if I totally needed. But I didn't want to. She befriended me faster than anyone else on the ship. Except maybe Coffee.

Oh, Coffee. I couldn't stop thinking about her.

"Oh, my stars," Vanilla said from the top of the steps as the dragons were led below her into the cargo section of the ship. Sage stood there beside her with big eyes and a suspect grin. She was impressed, no doubt. But she also clearly had plans for the creatures that would serve her own interest.

"I have a scanner that has been adapted to work on animals and alien lifeforms," Vanilla explained to Cinnamon after she descended to the lower level. She kept glancing at the faces of the two dragons as they rested on the floor, but she did not address them directly. "I can probably diagnose their injuries fairly well. However, treating them will not be the same as what I can do with humans. Their biology is not on file so I can't just regenerate their tissue quickly. It will take time for the computer to analyze them before I can do much in the way of healing. Except for the basics, of course. We can bandage their lacerations and stop the external bleeding. Reduce swelling where we should. Things like that."

"I understand," Cinnamon replied. "I will explain it to them. Just having a safe place to rest will help them right now. Thank you, Vanilla."

The divinely sexy doctor glanced around a bit more then slumped her shoulders. She looked into Cinnamon's eyes and asked, "Is Coffee really gone?"

My Cinnamon girl nodded as her face flooded with tears. Vanilla then pulled her into a comforting embrace as they cried together.

"I'm so sorry," I heard Dawynda mutter from where her snout was resting on the floor.

That's when I noticed Honeysuckle standing over by her maintenance station. She had a shocked expression at hearing the news of losing her best friend. Her eyes were welling up, but the tears weren't flowing yet. Instead, her body started trembling, as did her lower lip.

I took a deep breath and tried to right myself so I could go to her. She needed my comfort. But she bolted past us and up the stairs. I tried to follow but my energy was too low to keep up. Sage stepped aside and let her go by without much compassion apparent in her expression. At least she wasn't standing there with one hand on her fat hip like she tended to do.

"Whenever this is all under control," Sage said quietly to me and Strawberry. The redhead was following me up the stairs. Maybe not to comfort Honeysuckle, though. "We need to get everything loaded back into the ship," Sage told us.

I nodded, then remembered Dawynda's list. We had more things to acquire before we could take off with them, if that is what they chose to do. "We need to get some food for them if they decide to stay onboard."

"I can help with that," Strawberry said as she stepped up to my side and placed one delicate hand on my shoulder.

"You," Sage looked at her, "have enough work to do already inside the ship."

"I can do both," the redhead stated stubbornly.

Sage took a deep breath and slowly released it. Her attitude then came down a notch. She didn't like seeing her second in command taking my side so often. But she needed to maintain control. Over her emotions and of her crew.

"So be it," she replied. "But the faster the better." Then she sauntered away in her typical style.

Strawberry turned and pulled me to her in a soft embrace. She was almost a foot shorter than me, so her arms went around my waist as her head rested against my chest. I pulled her to me and instinctively placed my face on the top of her head. Her strong berry scent was both mesmerizing and arousing. I shook my head to clear it away.

"I'm so sorry for your loss," Strawberry said genuinely as she gently pulled away.

"Me, too," I answered. "But someone needs to comfort Honeysuckle right now. I don't imagine you want to do that."

Strawberry looked angered and offended for the briefest of moments. It confirmed my suspicion that there was definitely a significant barrier between them. But the look faded quickly as she shook her head and apologized. That was a better reaction than I had even hoped for. I needed to capitalize on it.

"What is it between you two?" I asked.

Strawberry shook her head more urgently. "Not now, Kash. One day soon I will tell you the story. Maybe she will tell her side first, if you push her. But we have other things to worry about right now. In fact, you should consider letting her be for a while."

That sounded like an awfully bad idea. However, I didn't always understand women. More than a few times I made things worse by not leaving them alone. But this did not seem like that type of situation.

"I need to at least check on her," I answered.

"Of course."

I released my hands from her shoulders and walked down the hall towards Honeysuckle's room. The door was closed, as expected. It did not open as I walked up. It never did. So, I tapped my knuckles against it. With all the technology on this ship I was surprised than none of the quarters had a doorbell, or even a camera to see who was knocking.

I tapped again and pressed my face to the door to tell her it was me. *Please let me in.* The rooms were soundproof to the point that you pretty much had to have your mouth against the door for the vibrations to get through to the other side. I was about to repeat my request when the door slid out of the way, nearly taking my face with it.

Honey was standing just inside the door. Her face, chest and neck were all wet. She lunged for me as soon as the door was out of the way. I held her tightly to me as we both began sobbing again. I had no words of comfort, though. Coffee meant a lot to both of us for different reasons. I was certain that any words that I could have shared were already conveyed in our desperate embrace.

"Can I sleep with you tonight?" she asked as she loosened her grip enough to peek up at me. In that moment she looked more like a sad daughter or younger sister than a lover. I nodded my approval before thinking that she might not be the only one sharing my bed tonight. Honey must have registered that thought at the same time. "Cinnamon can sleep on one side and me the other," she suggested.

"I would like that very much," I told her.

I pulled her to me and kissed the top of her head. Her white hair was so silky it felt like delicate feathers against my lips. Then I remembered that I had work to do. When I told her such, she announced that she had better get back to work, too.

"You can rest a bit more, if you want," I told her.

"No," she whispered. "Your hug was what I needed at the moment. And I'll be in your arms again tonight. We need to get this ship off this planet before anything else terrible happens. I am so done with this world."

It took some coordination and some cargo plan adjustments to accommodate the dragons. Curled up they took no more space than one cube. But it wouldn't be fair to keep them confined that way. As they began to regain their health and energy, they would need some walking around room. Otherwise, they'll be venturing upstairs or into the engine room. That should probably be avoided.

Vanilla was able to expedite her analysis process by checking to see how certain treatments would affect the dragons. Things that would be essential procedures if they were humans. Only half could be cleared by her medical computer as more than ninety percent risk free. So, she tried those as she waited for more information. Both Dawynda and Gako expressed that there were some unusual feelings as Vanilla went about her business. Cinnamon and I both had to be present to keep the dragons calm should they experience any pain. An hour later both patients were starting to feel better but still badly in need of rest.

"We all need rest," Sage told us. "We have a big day tomorrow. We'll run through the hull tests as quickly as possible and launch this ship."

There should have been cheers all around, but we were still in mourning. We could only get so excited without becoming offensive, so our enthusiasm was contained. It wasn't like any of us wanted to stay put. Not even I felt that way anymore. I had most of the girls on my side, Teddy was proving to be a particularly useful helper, and now two dragons. I didn't need to wait any longer.

I went to sleep with a beautiful young woman on each side, my arms around them as they slept on my chest. I wished the three-in-a-bed scenario happened under different circumstances. I had sexual experiences with both of these women and felt they were more than agreeable to having more in-depth adventures in the future. But this certainly wasn't the time.

I sang one of my songs to myself, but it was half-hearted in the wake of Coffee's tragic death:
If you're out there
Somewhere feeling lonely,
You're not the only one,
I like to double the fun.

I was worn out from the day's activity and fell asleep right after them. Between all the work and the battle against the orange dragons my energy was completely depleted. I must have slept longer than I thought because a knock at the door woke me. We must be running extremely late if someone had to come get us.

I slipped out of the tight configuration as best I could but there was no way not to wake them. I told them to go back to sleep while I answer the door, knowing that they probably wouldn't. They both sat up and watched as the door slid aside to reveal Sage standing there. She didn't seem the least bit shocked to find the girls in my bed.

"Kash," she said with a serious tone. "I need to talk to you. Privately."

CHAPTER TWENTY-SIX:

"We have a problem," Sage said quietly. She didn't whisper because it would mean leaning closer for me to hear. That would mess up her dominant persona. She almost grabbed me by the arm to lead me into the control room, then transitioned over to a hurry-up gesture instead.

"What kind of...?" I began to ask, quickly waking up due to the alarmed expression she was giving me.

"The hull," she answered. "It will not pass the tests this morning."

"Are you sure?"

"Yes," she answered stubbornly. "And we can't send anyone outside again to do the necessary repairs. The man with the orange dragons has returned with more."

I heard thumping on the roof of the ship to support her claim. I didn't want to face them again, especially without a healthy duo of my own dragons.

"We need to launch, but we can't leave the atmosphere," she explained the reason for this hush hush meeting.

"Shouldn't Strawberry and Honeysuckle be in on this...?"

"No," she said plainly. "This is between you and me. Once we are in the air the rest of the crew will have to deal with it. I just need you as the pilot to know ahead of time. This way I won't have to override your controls and fly this bird myself."

I thought about it, but it was too much to calculate all the possible angles she might be playing. But if the hull was not a hundred percent would it be safe to fly at all? Isn't the atmosphere harder on the ship than the void of space? I started to say as much to her before she cut me off, once again.

"We can deal with an air leak, if needed," she explained. She must have interpreted my facial expressions to know what I was thinking. "We won't get high enough to face any real danger anyway. Once we get going the computer will send us readings that include a discouragement from attempting to leave the atmosphere. We'll pick a more suitable place to land and make our remaining repairs. It will be a short stay. Hopefully, there is a desert or other type of land that will lack predators."

I agreed to do as she said. I could always change my mind later or reveal this conversation to the rest of the crew if the timing was right to make my final move against Sage. At this point though, I wasn't sure how things would play out. I hated being one step behind her. Sometimes it felt like I might actually be several steps behind.

I watched as Sage walked to the captain's chair and pressed the full ship intercom button. "Prepare for launch," she told everyone. "You have ten minutes to get in position, then twenty minutes for the checklist. We launch in thirty minutes."

There was a scurry of activity as we all got cleaned up, dressed and in position. We told Teddy and the dragons to brace themselves, though I was hoping the lift off would be smooth. Hopefully, I could pull off a gentle landing as well. Most of my simulator repetitions were spent on docking with a station instead of landing on a planet's surface, but how hard could it be? The computer actually did most of the work, especially at the very end.

Everyone was seated on the bridge. I thought that Honeysuckle might be positioned in the engine room instead, but this was not a test. We were able to raise the ship off the ground and into the air. Most of the crew still expected us to leave the planet and venture through space, too. The mechanic was required to be in the control room with the rest of us.

I slid into the pilot's seat front and center. The navigation station on my left was empty. That was Sage's job, and she would be doing that from the raised captain's chair directly behind me. The seat to my right was also empty. That's where Coffee would handle all communication related business. I didn't let my eyes, or heart, linger too long on her absence.

To Sage's left was Strawberry. She was primary eyes on all systems and in charge of the checklist for pre-launch. Honeysuckle was positioned behind her next to the door. On the right of the captain was Cinnamon. Cargo was her job, but she served as a redundant set of eyes on systems checks before take-off and specific performance monitoring during flight. Vanilla was behind her and responsible for life support first and foremost. Once we cleared the atmosphere, if that was what we were actually going to do, she would be dismissed from the bridge.

I trusted Cinnamon to keep an eye on Gako, Dawynda and Teddy for me via monitors and vitals readings. I would need to be focused entirely on flying the ship. There could be no distractions for me. Especially since this was my first time.

The knocking on the roof of the ship continued as we finished the pre-launch checklist. Sage scrolled through available camera angles to show the fat bearded guy leading more than a dozen dragons in a futile attack on the ship. Honeysuckle was sure that they couldn't cause any real damage. The man and two of the beasts were trying to get in the back door while a few others were biting and clawing at the engine exhaust ports.

"Those fuckers are going to die quick," Strawberry announced. "Once we fire up the engines someone will have some roasted dragon prepared for them to eat."

"They like their meat raw," Cinnamon announced, deflating the humor of the system's analyst's joke.

Then silence as I waited for the green light on my station. I had completed my portion of the checklist several minutes ago and was trying to stay focused. It was hard to do while wondering what to do about Sage's command to not leave the atmosphere and safely land elsewhere. Under what conditions would I reveal that to the crew? What could happen to make me disobey that order? If the computer returned an all-good on the hull report once we got airborne, should I still follow the command to land?

As acting captain, Sage had the ability to override pretty much everything from her seat. She would need to have that fat ass wrestled from the chair for me to be successful in a rebellion while in flight. I had to do as she said. When the time came for her to give the order to not leave the planet, I would act like I already knew. Then the girls could figure out on their own that she had given the order ahead of time.

"Cleared for take-off," Strawberry finally said.

All crew members were in the same room, but behind me. Their eyes should be glued to their monitors, but I felt like they were all staring at the back of my head. Sage had stopped switching the camera angles on screen and let it remain on the forward view. It had a good effect on my focus. Seeing where I was going, just like in a car on Earth, made a big difference. Maybe in space it wouldn't, but with ground, hills and trees so close, it certainly did.

We didn't bother to watch the dragons at the rear of the ship get toasted or obliterated when the engines rumbled. Or at least I didn't. All my attention was on the task at hand.

All lateral movement thrusters were active, as were the lift off jets below the ship. I merely had to follow a sequence before taking manual flight control. Elevate the ship to thirty meters minimum. Perform some very slight horizontal movements to test thruster performance and accuracy. Then engage the main forward motion engine.

My first shuffle to the side was a little too quick. It actually made me lean to the side a bit. I was sure that the others felt it, too. But no one said anything. Perhaps they were all holding their breath. I certainly was.

When I engaged the main thruster, nothing happened. At least I didn't feel anything. So, I tapped the forward virtual button on my display. There was the slightest of jerks backward into the seat, then a smooth movement. I could see the ground moving below us to confirm everything was going according to plan. We were headed toward the cliff, so I adjusted slightly to the right to keep me from panicking.

I used my left hand to gently slide the incline adjustment upward as I went. Slowly from zero to thirty percent. At the same time my right hand worked the acceleration slide until it reached the one thousand meters per second plateau. At that point, a second slide appeared above it on my screen to allow for faster movement. The slower scale then faded from the screen over the next few seconds and was replaced by a button that simply asked *Slower?*

Once I achieved a height of a thousand meters, I gently eased the ascent slide to zero while doubling our speed. The terrain was moving very slow below us, but it wasn't as easy to see. Green misty clouds greatly reduced our visibility. On my monitor, though, I had two sections showing me what lied ahead. One was like a simulated forward camera angle, and the other from above. The top view had readings for how close each hill or massive red tree was from my current altitude. We were well above everything nearby before the mysterious atmosphere began to mess with the sensors.

I had done it. I got us safely off the ground and into the air. I released my breath as silently as I could. I half expected to hear a sigh of relief from those behind me, but I didn't. I was tempted to turn and see everyone's expressions, but that would reveal my lack of confidence. I couldn't have that.

"Engines are performing well," Honeysuckle declared with a touch of pride. "Just a three percent flux in the left rear, and an eight percent in the middle right lateral thruster."

"Don't worry about that, Kash," Sage told me. "The computer will adjust easily for small variances like that."

"I confirm engine report," Strawberry announced with professionalism. "Hull reports are coming back good as well."

"Really?" Sage asked. I could hear just a touch of concern in her voice. No hull problem, no reason to land again. "That is surprising."

"No, it is not," Honeysuckle responded defensively.

"Based on pre-launch analysis," Strawberry stated. "It is unexpected. Two sections were showing a twenty to thirty percent chance of issues once we reach a higher speed."

"Well, then let's do that, Kash," Sage said.

"How much faster?" I asked. Looking out the screen was beginning to give me a feeling like I was driving through a dense fog. I did my best to focus on the screen display instead, though its reliability had diminished as we gained altitude.

"Double," the acting captain ordered. "Then wait for a report. If all is good, we'll double again."

I slid the velocity guide to double our speed. I couldn't feel anything but the number on my display doubled and it looked like the screens showed increased movement. I waited a few seconds for a report. Should I have announced that I doubled the speed already? It wasn't mentioned in my training, but they always did that in the sci-fi flicks back on Earth.

A moment later Strawberry gave us an update. "The section on the bottom hull has cleared. The section on the front right where Koradd's, um I mean Kash's quarters are, is showing an increased risk."

"That can't be," Honey muttered from the back left. She had spent so much time repairing that section. I was with her for part of it.

"Forty seven percent chance that we rip a hole before we leave the atmosphere," the redhead told her.

"That's not good," Sage then said. I wasn't sure if anyone else could hear the satisfaction in her voice.

"Life support will struggle with that breach," Vanilla announced. The sound of her elegant voice was rare in the control room. "But we can seal that room and be just fine once we are in space."

"I don't know about that," Sage told her.

"Excuse me?" the doctor replied. She didn't sound too offended, but she was clearly asking why her analysis was being challenged.

"All things considered," Sage said. "We shouldn't risk it. We just patched the ship together and left in a hurry. We'll need to land to perform repairs."

"What?" Strawberry asked in controlled shock. So, she was left out of the loop on this one. I wondered what that meant for me.

"The hull will hold!" Honeysuckle raised her voice in anger. "Tell her, doc! We'll be fine. Let's go already."

Vanilla remained quiet. She was more of a stickler for following orders than even Strawberry.

"My decision has been made," Sage announced. "Kash, take us thirty degrees to the right and reduce speed as we look for a good place over there to land."

I couldn't help but turn back toward the others. Everyone was indeed looking at me. Some were bewildered, others concerned. Honeysuckle was angry and Sage was satisfied. I paused long enough to give Sage concern before nodding. Then I turned back around and did as I was ordered.

"We're leaving this land mass," Cinnamon informed us. "Nothing looks that great for a landing before we reach the sea."

"How is the hull looking Strawberry?" Sage asked.

"The hull will hold!" Honeysuckle nearly shouted.

"Should be fine if we don't accelerate too much," the system's girl replied, ignoring Honeysuckle's outburst.

At Sage's command I continued to fly in that direction over the sea. I increased speed again without any repercussions, but we spent at least a half hour over water before spotting another land mass again. Some of the girls were getting antsy about the possibility of landing on water. There was a murmur that we should turn back. But as Cinnamon had told us, there weren't any perfect landing spots back there. With my limited experience I preferred to have a safe margin for error. A big open field would be lovely, if we could find one.

The new land mass was vastly different from the one that we left behind. No steep inclines or drop offs. More like rolling hills. I was sure we could find a reasonably flat area to touch down. I wanted to drop down a little to get the sensors more accurate. Then something flashed red on my screen and the ship shook like a turbulence of a plane. And we started veering to the left.

"Oh no!" Strawberry said, a rare hint of panic in her voice. "Left rear engine is failing!"

"Damn dragons!" Honeysuckle said. "That's not my fault!"

"The dragons couldn't have..." the redhead started to reply.

"It doesn't matter," Sage cut them off. "We need a spot to land now!"

Cinnamon then announced, "Fifteen degrees to the right and two kilometers ahead is the best choice according to the computer. Second and third choices are even farther."

"I'm struggling to turn right," I told them. I would push my finger along the screen, but it would vibrate and refuse to move the slide.

"The computer won't compensate for this big of a failure," Sage told me. "Do you need me to take control?"

"No!" I reacted immediately. There was no fucking way I was going to let her steal the glory of a safe landing. I'd rather crash than let her take over. "Just tell me what to.... Never mind. I've got it."

I remembered my training and reduced my speed. That gave me more steering ability. I tapped certain thrusters off to give the ship a tilt to the right. I could feel it in my seat like a plane turning to line up with the landing strip. That was basically what I was doing. Only I wouldn't need a runway.

"What in the stars?" Strawberry asked.

"It's fine," Sage told her. Of all the crew members besides me she was the only one with any pilot training at all. The basics had been part of her navigation courses.

Once I got to the clearing that Cinnamon pointed out I had to reengage the thrusters that I had turned off and shut down the right rear engine that was pushing us forward. I didn't quite get centered but there was plenty of space on all sides of the ship to not have to worry about landing at too much of an angle for comfort.

I dropped us straight down at a slow rate. Just five meters per second toward the end. During that time, the screen showed the location of dozens of rocks jutting upward out of the yellow grass. Some of them were more than three meters high, but narrow. I had to make horizontal adjustments three times, and a slight spin of the nose of the ship at the very end. Once within thirty meters of the ground the auto-land feature finally appeared on my screen. I tapped it gladly and let the computer set us down softly.

"Nice job, Kash," Cinnamon said as the impact with the ground was barely noticeable.

"Yes," Sage added. "You remembered your training well."

I chuckled as I got a Jedi Knight vibe from her statement. Then others commended me, and I nearly blushed at the appreciation.

"Air quality out there seems very close to the last place we landed," Vanilla announced.

"Crashed," Honeysuckle mumbled. The last location wasn't chosen. The ship had crashed.

"Whose fault was that?" Strawberry muttered her reply, lacking her typical professionalism.

"Any creatures out there?" Sage asked slightly louder to regain control of the room.

"Nothing of significant size," Cinnamon reported.

Sage clapped her hands on the console and asked, "Who wants to be the first one out?"

"I do!" I declared at the exact same time as Strawberry.

CHAPTER TWENTY-SEVEN

Teddy wasn't as excited about the idea of leaving the ship as I had expected. Part of that probably had to do with the news that we had never left the planet. His mind was already adjusting to what might happen once the ship reached a human station.

Strawberry and I decided to go ahead and put on a thin coat of the scent blocker just in case. It was the first time that we did so together. There was something about applying the paste to her petite but curvaceous body that got me aroused. I was having flashbacks to the sexual encounter that we had just recently.

"Your boner is impressive," Teddy whispered to me afterwards. "But more than slightly inappropriate under the circumstances. Do all human males have trouble focusing when their females are in heat?"

"I'm not in heat!" Strawberry turned so fast in outrage.

"I can smell you just fine," Teddy told her. "Mostly before you got covered with the mud, but still. It is clear that your body is craving sexual relations."

"Shut him up," Strawberry told me with wide eyes before she crossed her arms and gave my little friend a dirty look. She did not appreciate him ruining her game.

I hushed Teddy and told him to be quieter in the future with private information. I still wanted the intel, but there was no reason to tip off my sexual prey.

Strawberry got over the issue and addressed a new subject as soon as we exited the ship. I could tell that she already had the question prepared. "Did you already know that Sage was going to tell you to land again on this planet?"

"I did," I answered with an apologetic tone. "She approached me early this morning with it. I was waiting for the right time to rat her out, but it didn't play out that way."

"If this new partnership is going to work," she told me with a touch of my shoulder to gain eye contact. "We need to be more open with each other. You could have sought me out."

"Yeah?" I replied with a bit of an attitude. "Open like telling me what is between you and Honeysuckle."

"Oh," she replied as she came to a stop. "I can see what you mean. Well, it is nothing really. Her distaste with me is entirely different than my issue with her."

I stood there and waited for her to expand on the topic.

"She got upset with me because I had sex with her brother on her station when we recruited her to be part of the crew."

"What????"

"Yeah, I told her that I didn't know that he was her brother."

"Is that true?"

She bit her bottom lip as she smiled. It was seductive as all hell. "No. I did it on purpose as a power play. We used to do things that way before. Sage and me. But things are different now."

"Really?" I responded. She shrugged her soldiers and said no more. "What do you have against her?"

"Her negligence caused us to crash on this planet," she informed me like it was an established fact.

"Are you sure about that?" I asked. When she nodded, I told her that Honey suggested that someone had sabotage the ship instead. She looked puzzled but not convinced. At least it gave her something to think about. It wasn't a good time for a lengthy conversation on the matter. We were nearly to the end of the tunnel between the two engines as we slowly walked.

The ground we were walking on wasn't tremendously different than what we had experienced before. The yellow grass was denser and shorter, but remarkably similar in shade and blade shape as what we were accustomed. Beyond the hull, though, the scene was dramatically different. There were no trees close by. And the hills only rose maybe twenty or thirty feet above the valleys. That is why we selected this spot to land. Actually, the computer suggested it first.

I saw a green rat from about ten feet away. That was a new creature. It was over a foot long and scurried off when it saw us. You would think that just the ship coming down would scare off most wildlife. But then again, the touchdown was exceptionally soft and reasonably quiet.

Teddy had ventured ahead of us, surprisingly. I trusted his wits and instinct as much as anyone's. Add his sense of smell to that since he revealed Strawberry as being in heat.

"What is that?" Teddy asked pointing over to the side of the ship. We had to clear the rear corner in order to see it. It was one of the tall skinny rocks that we picked up on as we were landing. I even had to adjust a few times to avoid them. Only it wasn't really a rock.

It may have just been a rock at one time, but now it was a statue. Someone had carved it in great detail. It stood much taller than a human. Probably it wasn't to scale. But the form of the creature that it depicted was quite human-like.

"Oh, my stars," Strawberry uttered their most common exclamation these days as my jaw dropped. The statue was of a naked woman. Only not quite human.

The crew of this ship had some interesting body modifications. And I had been told that others went even more extreme. But this was well beyond anything that I ever heard of or even considered possible.

The long slender feet had three toes each, and a heel that was slightly raised like a paw of an animal would be. Thin legs that I would certainly consider sexy tapered out from the ankle until it reached the hip joint. There was a knee along the way, but it did not bulge out at all. And it was about two thirds of the way up the leg.

The depicted woman had wide hips, but in an attractive way. Then an extremely narrow waist. She was as sculptured as Sage. Next though, were the biggest round breasts that I had ever seen. With giant nipples that poked out several inches. Sucking on those would take some getting used to, I thought.

She had slender arms and a longer neck than a human would have. Three slim fingers on each hand with a tiny nub of a thumb. Her head was very much like ours, only with large, pointed ears. Even more so than Vanilla's. She had more alarming variances, though. Sprouting from her back was a pair of wings like an angel. She looked downright biblical in her still and rock-solid form.

"There are more," Teddy told us as he pointed to others spread throughout the field. "And they are all different."

One was wider and more muscular, but still feminine somehow. Another was down on all fours like she was grinding on the dance floor. Her fat ass would have been quite inviting for a number of male club goers. The third one had a tail and a nose that protruded like a dog. Or maybe a fox. She still managed to look elegant.

The last one that was close to the ship was the most shocking. She had bulky muscular legs with fur. I say *she* because her boobs were quite impressive on her short torso. As were her oversized lips and eyes. And the long flowing hair that nearly touched the ground. Upon further inspection, though, between her legs was a protrusion like a penis, fully erect and nearly as large as mine.

"Hah," Strawberry laughed outright. "I like this one," she said. I remembered then that she was bisexual. Of course, she would like a woman with a gigantic boner.

"I'm still waiting on my report," Sage's voice came through the speaker on our wrist communicators. "Are there any large animals or other concerns? Is it safe to do our repairs here?"

"I think so," Strawberry answered as she looked around the area beyond the statues. "But there are some interesting statues."

"Statues? Of what?"

"Girls," Strawberry snickered. "Naked girls. But not quite human."

"What do you mean?"

I pressed the button to reply as Strawberry eyed me with an ornery smile. "Sage, these statues may be of Gods or of their own kind. If the latter, this place was once populated with monster girls."

Thank you for reading Dragon Girls. A sequel is already available on Amazon. If you enjoyed the writing style and story, please check out other works of mine at rodzillabraun.com.

Writing a novel can often be challenging, requiring perseverance and intense focus. Along every step of the way I think of my readers and what they enjoy. Please take a moment to rate and review this novel on Amazon and Goodreads. Not only will it help me make adjustments, but your words could also assist other readers like you take a chance on this series.

I appreciate it.

Rodzil LaBraun

CPSIA information can be obtained
at www.ICGtesting.com
Printed in the USA
LVHW080154261121
704499LV00012B/829